"I'm not sweet. I'm trouble. Remember?" Hannah said.

"You can be both. And some trouble is worth getting into."

She grinned at him. "I think that's the best non-apology I've ever gotten."

He met her honey-brown eyes. Amusement faded from her face, uncertainty replacing it. As he took her in, really looked at her, the uncertainty in her expression mixed with awareness, and his throat grew thick.

Slowly, he grasped her chin and brought her mouth closer. There was something about her features, the lines and curves of her body, the fierceness of spirit, that lured him in.

He drew closer, stopping a hair's breadth from kissing her. "Sweet trouble," he whispered, aching to taste her.

A crash outside—the sound of glass shattering—had her spinning toward the window and Matt leaping up off the floor.

He looked out the window. Flames danced over the hood of his truck, like someone had thrown a Molotov cocktail.

WYOMING
RANCH JUSTICE

JUNO RUSHDAN

Harlequin

INTRIGUE

For all the first responders. Thank you for your service.

Harlequin®
INTRIGUE™

ISBN-13: 978-1-335-45688-5

Wyoming Ranch Justice

Harlequin Enterprises ULC
22 Adelaide St. West, 41st Floor
Toronto, Ontario M5H 4E3, Canada
www.Harlequin.com

Printed in U.S.A.

Juno Rushdan is a veteran US Air Force intelligence officer and award-winning author. Her books are action-packed and fast-paced. Critics from *Kirkus Reviews* and *Library Journal* have called her work "heart-pounding James Bond-ian adventure" that "will captivate lovers of romantic thrillers." For a free book, visit her website: www.junorushdan.com.

Books by Juno Rushdan

Harlequin Intrigue

Cowboy State Lawmen: Duty and Honor

Wyoming Mountain Investigation
Wyoming Ranch Justice

Cowboy State Lawmen

Wyoming Winter Rescue
Wyoming Christmas Stalker
Wyoming Mountain Hostage
Wyoming Mountain Murder
Wyoming Cowboy Undercover
Wyoming Mountain Cold Case

Fugitive Heroes: Topaz Unit

Rogue Christmas Operation
Alaskan Christmas Escape
Disavowed in Wyoming
An Operative's Last Stand

Visit the Author Profile page at Harlequin.com.

CAST OF CHARACTERS

Matt Granger—A military hero turned part-time rancher and campus chief of police at the Southeastern Wyoming University, where a killer is hunting victims.

Hannah Delaney—A strong-willed detective who goes undercover as bait to catch the university killer. Will the secret she's hiding threaten her ability to do her job?

Erica Egan—This journalist will cross any line for a scoop and to see her name in the byline.

Kent Kramer—Not the biggest fan of Hannah Delaney's, this detective is willing to help catch a killer.

Nancy Tomlinson—FBI profiler out at Quantico.

Victor Starkey—A sergeant with the campus police department.

Prologue

He'd waited as long as he could, holding back the urge until it took control. Tonight, he would sate the dark hunger gnawing at him and find some sense of relief.

Watching her, he licked his lips, excited and eager for their hookup. He had it all planned. Everything was in place and ready. The SUV. The syringe. The intimate hideaway where they'd have lots of privacy and time for him to play. She looked stronger than the others. Maybe she'd last more than a day or two. He had high hopes for this one.

Jessica logged off the computer in the university lab and began packing up her things.

Now. He threw a book in his backpack, slung it over his shoulder and hurried to beat her to the door without looking like he was rushing. The key to pulling it off, he'd learned the hard way, was in the timing. If he left behind her, then she'd be on the defensive, wondering if he was following her.

Leaving the place first—whether the lab, the café, the rec center—and then luring his prey to come to him had consistently been easier than shooting fish in a barrel and always got him his quarry without fail.

He pretended to hobble on the foot he'd Velcroed into the immobilization boot on his left leg. Shoving through the front door of the Southeastern Wyoming University computer lab, he stepped out into the cool late-night air. No worries about leaving his fingerprints; the seamless flesh-colored gloves solved that problem. He bent his head away from the camera and lowered the bill of his cap pulled over a shaggy ginger-colored wig.

Plenty of traps everywhere, but he was vigilant. He was prepared.

Making his way to the SUV he kept prepped for these special nights, he slowed down when he heard her leave the building and the door clicked shut. Anticipation slithered through him.

She was only a few feet behind him, drawing closer. He limped to his vehicle parked at the far end of the lot, near the alley she liked to use as a shortcut to the bus stop, where she was headed now, rather than take the long way around the block.

Dropping his bag and decoy keys on the ground, he swore loudly. He bent over and feigned struggling to pick up his keys, which he had slid beneath the car with his foot.

"Oh, man." Another curse flew from him as he glanced around, catching her eye. "Hey." He gave a quick wave with his right hand, ensuring she could see his other arm tucked in a sling like a broken wing, and she slowed. "Would you mind helping me a second?" he asked, and she stopped. He pushed the nonprescription glasses up on the bridge of his nose and limped a couple of steps, giving her a clear view of the medical boot. "If I get down there, I might not be able to get back up." Flashing a gentle smile, he fought the impulse to scratch the top of his lip, which itched from the fake mustache. He was anxious to shed the disguise. Even the colored contacts irritated his eyes.

Jessica glanced from side to side, then looked between the sling and the immobilization boot, deliberating.

She was perfect. Precisely his type. White. Slim. Blond. Dark eyes. High cheekbones. Pretty mouth. Only twenty-years-old. Easygoing. Not too wary.

He'd considered a few others, but she was his top pick for his next hookup. This was going to be his lucky night.

"This is what I get for trying to ride my bike more and do my part to save the environment," he said lightly, raising the sling. "Someone not paying attention hit me. I'll owe you one."

With a nod, Jessica headed toward him, making the mistake of thinking he wasn't a threat. "I'm the same. Even though my parents offered to help me buy a car, I either bike or take the Secure Ride," she said, referring to the public transportation bus service offered by the university.

Little did she realize that she'd never make it to the bus tonight.

"I would've taken the Secure Ride myself," he said. "But at the closest stop, there isn't a bench, and I'd have to stand while I wait for the bus. The doc told me to keep pressure off my foot." As she drew closer, he pulled the grin wider. His excitement over the risk of grabbing her was liquid fire in his veins. The burn was good. "I appreciate you helping me." He hid his right hand behind his leg, and the sling covered most of the other. Up close, someone could tell he was wearing gloves if they looked carefully. "Can I pay you back with a coffee or something at the Wheatgrass Café?"

Stepping within his reach, she flicked her hair over her shoulder, kicking up the sweet scent of her perfume. The smell reminded him of a previous hookup.

"No need." She narrowed her eyes at him for a second. "Hey, I know you. You're in my Mythology 101 class. I nearly knocked you down the other day." Her shoulders immediately relaxed. A smile tugged at her rosy lips.

Another key to success was to pick one of their classes. The larger, the better, where he could blend in, disappear. Simply sit in once or twice while in disguise. Orchestrate a meeting where they bump into him or vice versa. That first connection, the initial spark, made this moment when he snatched them so much easier because once they remembered him, it lowered their guard.

"Oh yeah," he said, filling his altered voice with pleasant surprise. "I didn't recognize you." The truth was, he'd memorized her face, the shape of her body, the way she moved. Fantasized about tonight a hundred times. "By the way, I'm Theodore Cowell. Just call me Theo." Introductions put them further at ease.

"Jessica Atkinson."

His next steps flew through his mind. *Take hypodermic needle from sling. Dose the girl. Grab her. Quick tussle—* they always fought and lost. *Pop trunk. Toss her in the vehicle. Handcuffs. Leg irons. Gag. Drive.*

He could do it in under a minute. His best record was twenty-two seconds. None had ever gotten away. By the time he got behind the wheel and sped off, the ketamine would hit her system, keeping her quiet for several hours. Once she woke up, then they'd party.

"Thanks again." He smoothed his palm over the slight bulge of the compact handgun tucked in the pocket of his lightweight jacket. He only carried it for insurance. Not that he had a problem killing an animal or a person by pulling the trigger—he was a hunter in every sense of the word and was even a long-range deadeye, capable of hitting a target one mile away. But using a gun to wrangle his prey would be cheating.

"Sure. No problem." She got down on her hands and knees and reached under the car for his keys.

Always worked like a charm.

Time slowed to a crawl. He looked around, sweeping the area once more, ensuring no witnesses lurked nearby. It was just the two of them. His heart throbbed with anticipation as he pulled out the hypodermic needle.

Chapter One

Hannah Delaney got off the Secure Ride bus operated by SWU, surprised it had arrived four minutes ahead of schedule. Hitching her backpack on her shoulder, she headed for the computer lab to work on a project.

At least, that was what she wanted people to believe.

Her police chief had given her the undercover assignment at the last minute after the University Killer suddenly resurfaced ten days ago, taking the life of twenty-one-year-old Madison Scott. For nearly the past decade, the murderer had struck on and off, always claiming three lives within a month, using the same MO before disappearing again.

Hannah had pored over the routines of the previous victims, zeroing in on things they'd had in common, and tried to recreate their lifestyle. She'd moved into on-campus housing, enrolled in a myriad of classes, frequented the Wheatgrass Café, rode the Secure Ride bus at night, hit the gym at the Sweetwater Recreation Center, biked during the day to downtown, shopped at the farmers market and caught live music at the local bar, the Watering Hole.

She still hadn't had a chance to swing by the computer

lab at night on a regular basis like some of the victims had done in years past. Fall semester had only been in session for less than three weeks. With all the new student events and socials, where a predator might be lurking, there simply hadn't been enough hours in a day to cover everything. She had to prioritize. The lab wasn't high on the list, since Madison Scott had never been there. Quite honestly, Hannah didn't understand why many students would use the campus computer lab these days when most had a personal laptop.

Time was running out. The killer was going to snatch his next victim soon. Only twenty days left for him to claim two more lives. Hannah only hoped she was doing enough to catch his eye. She'd do anything to spare someone else from being violated and murdered. Stopping monsters was her life's mission, the only way for her to atone and silence her demons. It drove everything she did—why she got up in the morning, became a detective, even why she kept everyone at a distance.

You'll find him. You have to.

Dressed in jeans, an open flannel button-down with a tank top beneath it, hair in a high ponytail to make her appear even younger, she blended in with any other student. The only thing to set her apart was the concealed gun in her inside-the-waistband holster at the five-o'clock position between her back and hip, and the small knife that was a part of her belt buckle.

She took the alley, a shortcut to the lab. There was no way for her to know for sure if any of the other victims had ever used this same route at some point leading up to their murder. It was smarter and safer to walk around the block to get to the lab, using the well-lit sidewalks, where a passerby might see something. Yet young people, not considering the fragility of their lives, tended to trade security for convenience.

People showed you who they were in subtle ways by their choices and preferences, which were almost as telling as a Myers–Briggs personality test if you watched someone for weeks on end. Whether they were cautious or carefree. Skeptical or trusting. Selfish or caring. Predictable or impulsive.

All the slain women had been described as kind, thoughtful, naive. Somewhat of a loner. Most importantly, creatures of habit.

Despite being the right physical type, this was where Hannah was at a disadvantage. Less than ten days wasn't long enough to establish a consistent routine, a pattern the University Killer could rely on. He not only chose his victims for their appearance, but she suspected he also stalked them to know precisely when and where to strike.

Two more women were going to die soon if she couldn't lure him in as the bait.

A soft scuffling sound came from the other end of the alley near the outskirts of the computer-lab parking lot. Whatever it was, it was bigger than a rat.

Hannah's gut tightened. She picked up her pace down the alleyway, sticking to the shadows of the wall. Straining to see in the dim light, she caught sight of a dark SUV, the back end of the passenger's side.

The trunk door popped open.

Someone grunted. More scuffling noises.

"What are you doing?" a woman asked, her voice frantic.

Two people stepped into partial view, but the dark SUV partly obscured them. A man wrestled with a blond woman, possibly in her early twenties. The man hit the blonde in the face, dazing her, and hauled her to the back of the vehicle.

Dropping her backpack, Hannah rushed forward. She drew her weapon from the holster.

"Police!" Hannah called out, holding the Glock in a two-handed grip, sighting down the barrel.

He whirled, pulling the woman up in front of him like a shield, one arm locked under her chin, pressed against her throat. With his other hand, he wrenched one of the blonde's arms clutched behind her back. An empty arm sling swung back and forth along his side. His gaze darted to the open trunk, and Hannah realized how close he had come to getting the young woman inside it.

"Let her go!" Hannah ordered. "Right now!"

Keeping the woman held tightly in front of him, he scurried backward around to the driver's side, dragging her along with him. Her nose was bloody. Her eyes were wide with fear. She clutched the arm over her throat, her feet shuffling in the direction she was being forced.

Easing around the rear of the vehicle, Hannah glimpsed inside the trunk. A chill ran through her. The interior of the cargo compartment was padded. A plastic tarp was laid out. Handcuffs and leg irons each dangled from a chain that had been bolted to either side of the trunk. On the breeze, the biting scent of bleach hit her. No license plate.

She rounded the back side, coming face-to-face with him. One clean shot was all Hannah needed.

"Release her, or I'll shoot." A complete bluff. Although an excellent markswoman, she didn't have a clear shot with the blonde being used as a human shield.

Between the shaggy hair, mustache, glasses and the way he hid his face behind the young woman's head, Hannah couldn't make out enough details to identify him, much less find the clearance to pull the trigger.

Yanking the woman another foot or two toward the driver-side door, he released the arm wrested behind her back and pulled something from his pocket. A semi-automatic pistol. "Drop your gun," he demanded, pressing the muzzle to the young woman's side. "Or I'll shoot her."

Hannah held her ground, keeping her weapon aimed levelly. "This isn't what you want," she said, taking a calculated risk. Killing his victims slowly after raping them was his MO. Taking her life in an impulsive act wouldn't satisfy him. Not only that, but he'd also lose his only leverage. "I don't think you're going to pull the trigger and kill her."

He eyed the car door. "Who said anything about killing her?" He jammed the muzzle into the woman's side so hard that she winced. "Drop it, or I start putting bullets in her."

Hannah hesitated. The need to put this monster down and end his nine-year-long killing spree was an ache in her soul. She might not get another opportunity if he slipped through her fingers now.

"The first one goes in her stomach," he promised.

Getting this woman out alive the only thing that mattered at the moment. Hannah glanced over her shoulder at the dumpster near the entrance to the alley. If he tried to shoot at her, she could make it there and duck for cover. She raised her palms with her gun vertical, barrel pointed up. Slowly, she set it down on the ground, never taking her gaze off him and the girl.

"Do you think I'm stupid? Kick it under the car."

She did as instructed, sending her weapon sailing beneath the SUV, only deepening the nasty twist in her gut spiraling into fear. Fear for the life of the young woman.

"Open the door," he snapped at the blonde, tightening his arm over her throat.

No matter what, Hannah wasn't going to let him get

away with another victim. Worst case, if he managed to get the girl into the car, she'd pull her backup weapon from her boot and blow out his tires. He wouldn't make it far.

With a shaking hand, the young woman grabbed the handle and opened it. Her eyelids grew heavy, and she swayed in his grip.

Was the hold on her throat choking her, cutting off her airway?

"Let her go!" Hannah took a tentative step forward. "She can't breathe."

"Don't you move. Not another step." He backed up, using the woman's body to block him. His arm loosened around her throat as he climbed into the vehicle, keeping the gun pointed at her side.

The woman swayed again, her head bobbing like she was going to keel over any second.

She'd been drugged. He must have dosed her with ketamine already.

The car engine roared to life while he kept the gun pointed at his hostage. "You'll have to choose. Me or her."

Choose? What does he mean?

He pulled the trigger, shooting the blonde in the side, and peeled off.

No!

The young woman staggered and slumped to the ground. The SUV sped across the parking lot, hitting the street. He turned the corner and sped away, tires squealing, as Hannah raced over to the young woman, knelt beside her and checked the wound.

Thankfully, the bullet had missed her stomach, but it had struck her just above the hip. The woman's brown eyes fluttered closed—a combination of the drugs and shock.

Hannah took off her shirt and applied pressure to slow

the bleeding. "Hang in there. You're going to make it." She whipped out her cell phone and called 911.

Once she heard sirens approaching, she wondered which campus officers would arrive on the scene.

She'd readily deal with any of them except for one—the SWU police department chief.

Matt Granger.

Chapter Two

Behind the wheel of his pickup truck, Matt Granger sped to the university campus with his teeth clenched. Since waking up that morning, he'd had a familiar tingle prickling his spine that forewarned him to prepare for trouble. It was his day off from the SWUPD. The bad feeling niggling him had made him consider going in, but he had coordinated a full load of work on the ranch with his cousins. Before he could relax with an ice-cold beer, a sergeant had called with news he'd been dreading.

A young woman had been shot during an encounter with a man they suspected to be the University Killer, and somehow a detective had been on the scene.

Trouble indeed—a subject in which he had plenty of experience. Truth be told, he was drawn to it…or rather, trouble was drawn to him. Good at seeing it coming and neutralizing it, a talent that had served him well during his time in the army as a Special Forces Operator. His job had been training and planning for the worst and then making sure it happened—to the enemy. After seeing too much carnage, he'd returned to his family's ranch, set between Laramie and Bison Ridge. The transition to the Laramie police force and later to campus law enforcement felt natural, even easy. He'd mistakenly thought that in the two small towns, where neighbors helped one another and everyone was so welcoming with open arms, things would be slower, quieter. Safer. Instead of bloodshed and loss, he'd finally find peace.

But whether he was in the army, with the LPD or the campus police, there was no escaping trouble and the death that always followed.

Matt pulled up to the headquarters of the SWUPD, located on the west end of campus, threw his truck in Park, and hurried inside. The department occupied five thousand square feet of the first floor of a parking garage, providing a modern, spacious facility for the law enforcement agency. He nodded hello to a couple officers.

One looked him over with raised eyebrows, making Matt consider how he must appear after sixteen hours of hard manual labor.

It had been his idea to expand his family's sources of revenue by designating a modest portion of the property to big game hunting. He'd taken the lead on building small cabins that could be rented to those looking to hunt or simply relax. Earlier, he and his cousins had been working on Sheetrock and wall texture since the wiring for the electricity had been finished.

Taking off his dark brown cowboy hat, he wished he'd had time to shower, or at least had the foresight to change his sweaty shirt, wash his face and grab a sandwich for the ride over.

Sergeant Lewis stood in Matt's office, talking to a woman—presumably the detective—seated in a chair that faced the desk. Lewis looked up, catching sight of Matt, and opened the office door for him.

"Evening, boss," Lewis said.

The woman pivoted in the chair, glancing over her shoulder at Matt and meeting his gaze. He swallowed a sigh.

Lewis gestured to her. "This is Detective—"

"Hannah Delaney," Matt interrupted, letting the spike of annoyance leak into his voice. The woman was the walking, talking epitome of trouble.

"Oh, you two know each other," Lewis said, surprise stamped on his face.

"Yeah." Hannah gave a curt nod to the officer while keeping her stare leveled at Matt. "We worked a case together before he quit being a detective with the LPD to hide out and play cop over here."

Matt tamped down a retort. He'd been through this rigmarole before, where a cop—usually a detective—hurled an insult at him for taking this position and he, stung by the icy disdain, inevitably went on the defense.

Little good it ever did him.

For some reason, when it came to Hannah, all her taunts teased in a way that reminded him he was not only a cop but also a man. "I forgot you could be so…" He let his voice trail off, realizing that finishing his statement wouldn't help the situation.

"Candid?" she offered.

He measured his words to mitigate the tension in the room. "I was going to say *blunt*. Hard-hitting." *Like a sledgehammer.*

He had no idea why he found that kind of sexy.

Lewis stood still and quiet, shifting an uncomfortable glance between them.

"Would you excuse us, Sergeant?" Matt guided Lewis to the door and closed it behind him. "What are you doing on my campus?" With Hannah, there was no telling. He crossed the room and dropped his hat next to his computer. Leaning on the edge of his desk, facing her, he noticed bloodstains on her white tank top. "And how are you involved in tonight's shooting?"

Sergeant Lewis had given scant details, as he hadn't had a chance to interview Hannah yet before he'd called Matt.

"For the past ten days," Hannah said, crossing her lean legs, "I've been on campus, pretending to be a new student named Helen Davis, in an undercover op to catch the University Killer."

Undercover? He had not seen that one coming.

"I'd been following the routines of the previous victims," she continued, "and came across him attempting to take his next. According to her student ID, she's Jessica Atkinson." Hannah ran through the events leading up to her 911 call.

The student was now being treated at the university hospital. Over the phone, Matt had instructed Lewis to send an officer to watch over her while she recovered.

"Where's your partner?" Matt asked.

"I'm solo on this."

The benefits of having her assigned to a case like this with a partner were obvious and numerous. So why was she working without backup?

He stiffened, hoping she hadn't gone rogue, taking it upon herself to do this outside official channels. If he had to describe Hannah in one word, it would be *firebrand*. And true to that nature, she was incendiary.

The only reason they had been put together on a case was because no one else wanted to work with her and he had lost his previous partner. To this day, he blamed himself for his death, even though the inquiry had found him not guilty of any wrongdoing.

"Why did they pick you?" He folded his arms across his chest. "And why alone?"

She narrowed her eyes at the questions.

Not that he meant them as an insult. One thing he didn't question was Hannah's extensive experience working undercover. If anyone could immerse themselves in a different world, become a different person—quickly—it was her. Yet something else about her that made him uneasy.

"The chief picked me," she said, meaning the chief of the Laramie police department, Wilhelmina Nelson. "She thought I would make the perfect bait."

Now that she mentioned it, Hannah did fit the profile of the previous victims—blond, trim, petite, dark eyes. Although she was twenty-eight, the right clothes, combined with her girl-next-door look and small stature, would make most guess she was no older than twenty.

"You should've notified me about your undercover operation." Matt scratched at the stubble on his jaw. "It's called *professional courtesy.*"

"Wasn't my decision not to notify you. Only following orders. If you have a problem with that, take it up with Chief Nelson."

The not-so-polite suggestion was only made to irk him. They both knew he wasn't going to go crying to anyone about this. "Any idea why you were given an order to cut me out of an op on my campus?"

"Three different campus police chiefs have tried and failed to catch this guy."

"And the LPD assumed I'd be the fourth?"

She gave him a one-shoulder shrug. "The University Killer has stayed two steps ahead of your department and evaded capture for almost a decade. There's a reason for that."

"What exactly are you implying? That the perp could be someone in the campus police department?"

"I didn't *imply* anything. I merely stated a fact. You have personnel who have worked here for ten-plus years. Three sergeants and a dispatcher. Everyone else in your department either attended SWU or has lived locally long enough to be a suspect. Have they been investigated?" she asked pointedly.

He flicked her an impatient glance, not caring for the second implication belying her tone. Did she think he was incompetent? "Of course they have, including the support staff."

Ten women had been violated and murdered over the years. The killer hadn't bothered to wear a condom when he'd raped his victims, leaving behind his DNA, and had put a queen of hearts playing card with the eyes scratched out on their corpses.

Matt had only recently taken over as chief. Still, the department's failure to find the killer weighed heavy on him. He'd hoped that the killer would be dead by now or too old to resurface. But as soon as the body of Madison Scott had been discovered—the first under his watch—it had taken him a week to investigate every single person in the department.

"I took the added precaution of getting everyone to take a polygraph test." It wasn't admissible in court and wasn't foolproof, but merely asking them to take it told him a lot if any refused. Mostly it gave him another opportunity for someone to slip up. As a detective, he'd even had a suspect confess once when questioned about how nervous he'd been during the test. "All their alibis have been checked, but two officers didn't have one," Matt admitted.

Hannah narrowed her eyes to slits. "Who are they?"

Hesitant to share that information, he knew not disclosing it would only further raise her suspicions.

"Officer Laura Jimenez," he said, and the tension in Hannah's face eased slightly at the mention of a woman. "And Officer Carl Farran. He would've been twelve at the time of the first murder, and he readily agreed to DNA testing when he didn't have to." Matt had cleared every other employee in the SWUPD. "I realize Chief Nelson suspects there are bad apples in every department, but I hope you don't share the same tainted view." He was willing to make an exception for Chief Nelson. She'd been brought into the Laramie Police Department for the express purpose of cleansing it of all the corrupt officers, and there had been plenty buried deep. More than enough to require help from the division of criminal investigation—the DCI—under the Wyoming State Attorney's General Office. No one was prepared for the vile things that case brought to light, such as a crooked lieutenant who sold the personal information of every officer in the department, endangering families, putting the lives of kids at risk. The worst part was, the seller had never been tracked down. "My officers aren't dirty, and they're certainly not serial killers."

"My, my, Matt, you seem a bit touchy regarding the subject."

To say he was sensitive on the issue would be an understatement. Not only had he worked for the LPD and had friends who had turned out to be crooked, but his cousin, Holden Powell, had gone through a scandal after his boss, the previous sheriff, turned out to be the worst of the worst when it came to corruption. For a long time, Holden had to deal with people gossiping, giving him the side-eye, wondering if he was guilty by association or how he could be so blind as to miss it.

It lit a fire under Matt to ensure his department was above board. "A dirty cop, much less a murderer hiding behind a badge, is a subject that should make any officer worth their salt touchy."

Her jaw hardened. "The campus police have turned up no leads, no solid suspects and no matches to the DNA the killer left behind. He just keeps slipping through your fingers like grains of sand."

Frustrated by the same thing, Matt had submitted the killer's DNA to a publicly accessible genetic-genealogy-testing service. More than one hundred users had matched as a distant relative, possibly as close as a third cousin. It would take four to six months of research to narrow it down to a pool of people who could be the University Killer. He had a retired investigator from the DCI working on it, unbeknownst to anyone in his office. He was keeping this information on a need-to-know basis. Eventually, the murderer would be caught; it was simply a matter of time, which he didn't have.

"You're not faring much better on your own," Matt said. "He slipped through your fingers tonight, didn't he? You're always the daredevil, but this was reckless. And what do you have to show for it besides a wounded victim?"

She jumped to her feet, still not coming eye level even with him sitting on the edge of the desk. Putting her hands on her slim hips, she drew closer, grazing his knee with her thigh. "Better wounded than dead. That's what she'd be if I hadn't been here undercover. This op was dangerous, sure. Not reckless. Maybe you've been playing cop too long on campus to remember the job can be hazardous."

He took a breath, not wanting to argue with her, especially when she had a legitimate point: Jessica Atkinson was alive and safe thanks to Hannah. "If you'd had backup, we might have him in custody."

"Backup would've meant a partner tailing me. This guy is really good. His setup was sophisticated. The fake arm sling and leg boot. Padded trunk to muffle noise. Handcuffs and leg irons. Which were just an added precaution because he drugs his victims before he even gets them in the vehicle. And the trunk reeked of bleach. A sign he's careful not to leave behind DNA in the vehicle. He would've spotted a partner. Maybe even sensed I was undercover as bait to trap him if someone had been shadowing me."

Hard to disregard Hannah's instincts or the fact that she had gotten more details about the way this guy operated than anyone else had in nearly a decade. Not that he liked how Chief Nelson had made Hannah bait, left to fend for herself with no backup, and had cut him out of the loop about an op on his campus. But whether it had been reckless or clever for her to be out there alone, he was no longer so sure.

"The killer never used a gun before that we know of," he said, looking for a way to get on better terms with her. "Thanks to you, we'll have ballistics."

"If only I'd had a little more time to lure him in," Hannah said, the regret in her voice palpable. "I'm sure he would've gone for me."

Half of him hoped that wasn't true despite the need to put an end to the killings. No victim had escaped the University Killer. Until tonight. The idea of this twisted psychopath setting his sights on Hannah, regardless of her training, had unease stirring in his blood. When they'd worked together and he'd seen firsthand the cavalier risks she took, which had ironically also made her successful, it'd triggered his protective instincts. Something she had made clear she didn't appreciate.

Not that he could help it or was sexist in any way. The military had programmed him to protect his country, his teammates and those in need, and to be merciless in that endeavor.

He got up and went around to the other side of his desk, putting ample distance between Hannah and himself. "Well, your cover is blown now since he got a good look at you. I trust you're not going to request to be taken off the case."

Her honey-brown eyes sparkled with a definite challenge. "You'd trust correctly."

One of the things he admired about Hannah was her spirit, her *never back down no matter what* attitude. It also worried him because one day it might get her killed.

He dropped into his chair, physically exhausted while adrenaline kept his mind sharp. "My department is going to continue investigating as well," he said. "To avoid wasting resources and duplicating effort, it only makes sense to work together from here on out. We'll make better headway faster. Besides, you could use a partner on this."

"Don't you mean, *campus police* could use a detective?"

Swallowing another sigh, he grinned. "My *advancement* to chief doesn't make me any less of a detective."

She rocked back on her heels, her face wary. "I hope you're not suggesting that you and I work together."

In his mind, there was no question about it. "As a matter of fact, I am. Is there another officer in my department who you think is more qualified? Who can keep up with you?" *Who won't let you run roughshod over them?* "Or who you can trust to have your back despite your brash risk-taking tendencies?"

Averting her gaze, Hannah smoothed a hand over her ponytail.

That was the first time he'd ever seen her speechless, and he relished being the one to have caused it. "What do you say? Unless you need to get permission from your chief before you can decide."

Straightening, she looked up at him. "I'm authorized to do what's necessary to get this guy, but I think it would be better if it was me and another *full-time* detective working this case."

Three irksome implications in one conversation. She was really trying to strike a nerve. Getting close, too. Maybe she wanted him to concede and turn over the case to the LPD.

Never one to shirk his duty, no way that was happening. The killer was targeting women on his campus, making it his responsibility. Detective Delaney would just have to deal with him.

"I'm not rusty." He'd been in the position of campus police chief for only a year. "I'll have Sergeant Starkey, my number two, manage the day-to-day stuff here, and then you'll have me all to yourself full-time," he said, knowing it was the last thing she wanted.

Her eyes flashed with annoyance, but a slight flush colored her cheeks.

Did he get under her skin the same way she did his?

For a few seconds, she just stared up at him. "The less time I spend with you, the better."

As he suspected. He wished he could say the feeling was mutual. She was a tough nut to crack. But the more she gave him a hard time, the more he itched to break past her shell to understand her better.

Being around her had him questioning whether he'd gotten it wrong. Maybe he was attracted to trouble.

"I get I'm not your first choice, or even on your list of choices." He wondered if anyone would make the cut on who she'd want to work with. She was such a loner. "But I thought we made a pretty good team on the cartel case."

A branch of a notorious Mexican cartel had set up shop practically in their backyard, processing and distributing fentanyl and methamphetamine. They had managed to find it and shut it down. No easy feat, with both of them nearly dying in the process, but she couldn't deny they'd been effective.

Hannah frowned. "Yeah, I suppose we did," she said, as if agreeing to eat a bowl of broken glass.

Good thing he didn't have a fragile ego. "I want this guy as badly as you do." Probably more. Every woman taken from his campus, violated and murdered, was one more to keep him up at night. "I think we can stop him. One more case together?"

After a long moment, she nodded her acquiescence. "Fine. I guess we're partners again. Stuck together for the sake of the greater good."

Could she look any less enthused?

Then again, of course she could. This was Hannah Delaney.

"Lucky me." His voice was thick with sarcasm. "Look, the sooner we catch this guy, the sooner you can go back to working solo."

"Just the way I like it." She stuffed her hands in her pockets. "But let's get one thing straight—I'm not following your lead or playing it safe this time."

As if she had before. Refraining from rolling his eyes, he gave his head a little shake in disbelief.

"To nail him," she said, her demeanor turning steely, "we have to do it my way."

Why was he not surprised? "I would expect nothing less."

But following her lead didn't mean he was going to abandon his good judgment.

This time around, he'd make sure they compromised and acted like partners. It was the only way for them to avoid another close call with death.

Chapter Three

For the past several hours, he'd been unable to sleep. Unable to eat. All he could think about was Jessica. Her sweet mouth. Her pretty face. Her perky breasts. Her lean legs. He pictured her stripped of all her clothes and having his way with her.

But he'd lost her because of that devious cop. She'd ruined his hookup. And he'd needed it so badly.

Anger and frustration ran riot inside him, tangling and swelling into a seething mass until he trembled from the force it. He'd been denied his satisfaction. The release he craved.

Swearing, he pounded a fist on the wood railing of his front porch and stared at the flames in the firepit. His head was throbbing. Maybe he should call in sick today and lick his wounds, even though it was better to stick to a routine the day after nabbing one of his dates.

Tried *to nab but didn't quite make it.*

Last night was a mere setback. Not defeat. He was not a loser, and he would not sulk.

He was going to fight for what he wanted. Take it with no remorse.

But missing a painstakingly planned hookup stirred other emotions inside him, ones he knew for certain he shouldn't dare entertain. Like finishing what he'd started with Jessica.

No, no. No! Too risky.

He had to focus on the next step. Moving forward.

But this growing need could destroy him if he didn't do something—and soon.

His mind careened back to the cop. The slender blonde. With dark eyes. Curves in all the right places. The one who had been undercover, acting like a student. He'd noticed her. How could he not? She stood out. But he'd had others on his carefully cultivated list.

Yes, the list. Stick to the others already chosen.

He'd take a different girl. With everything going on around campus, this week was best. The timing would be perfect.

But what about the pesky cop?

He had to teach her a lesson. Punish her for the sin of disrupting his process. Toy with her. Torture her.

Then he'd kill her, too.

Smiling, he walked down the porch steps, over to the firepit, and squeezed more lighter fluid onto the flames. The fire roared higher. Smoke curled around him. He picked up the disguise he'd shed from the ground and tossed it into the blaze.

Sometimes less was more, anyway. Glasses and contacts weren't necessary. One thing he was good at—had always been quite skilled at, even as a child—was becoming a chameleon. Though the loss of the sling and orthopedic boot hurt. He'd grown accustomed to using them to lure in his prey.

He'd gotten lazy. Complacent. Now he'd have to come

up with a new way to capture his birdies. He went back up to the cabin's porch.

Settling back in a rocking chair, he stared out over the woods that ringed the edge of his property. He loved the forest. Being out here alone never failed to calm him, to steady his thoughts. Rocking in the chair, taking in the green landscape, he considered the best way to achieve his goals.

Cops hated losing. Getting bested by the enemy. He smiled, now knowing exactly how to proceed.

Not only would he beat that harpy at this sport, but he was also going to humble her, break her, make her wish she had never messed with him. The thought of it gave him such sweet satisfaction.

First, he had to figure out who the hell she was. Wouldn't be hard.

With no idea that he was coming, it'd never occur to her that she should be the one hiding from him.

Chapter Four

Regret flared inside Hannah as she watched the forensic artist finish a drawing of the University Killer. Last night's events replayed in her head. Bleach. Handcuffs. Plastic tarp. How close she had gotten to stopping him but had ultimately failed.

Now that psychopath was still on the loose, looking for his next victim.

The forensic artist turned the sketch pad around to show Jessica Atkinson. "Is this him?"

"Yes, that's what he looked like," the young woman said from her hospital bed, staring at the sketch of her attacker. "You got all the details right." A shiver ran through Jessica, and she pulled the blanket up to her neck with a wince.

According to the surgeon, if the bullet had hit her two inches higher, she might not be alive. Once she recovered, and after some physical therapy, she'd be able to walk without a limp. In her bloodwork, they'd found the drug GHB, gamma-hydroxybutyrate, also known as liquid ecstasy. Not only was it a common, illegal date-rape drug, but it was also the same one that had been found in Madison Scott's system. Now they knew the University Killer used GHB in the abduction of his victims as well as throughout the time he held them captive up until he murdered them.

The forensic artist, who worked freelance for local law enforcement, lowered the sketch pad. "You did great, Ms. Atkinson. I only drew what you described."

Hannah took a quick picture of the drawing with her phone.

"You can drop it off with Sergeant Starkey at the station," Matt said to the artist. "I want to get his image out there for everyone to see before noon."

Little good it would do them. "It's a disguise," Hannah said to Matt, keeping her voice low. "He's only going to change it."

Jessica grimaced at the comment.

Hannah sighed. Guess her voice hadn't been as low as she thought.

Cupping her elbow, Matt ushered her off to the side of the room. His grip was firm, and the heat of his palm seeped through the sleeve of her blazer. She gritted her teeth to keep from squirming.

Across the room, the artist uttered something comforting to the young woman that made her nod, her eyes brightening with hope.

Hannah couldn't remember the last time she'd *felt* hope, much less inspired it.

Once they reached the window, she jerked her arm free of his hand.

At six-five, Matt stood a foot taller than her. Dark haired. Overly muscled. A rough-looking part-time cowboy.

They'd worked together when he was a distinguished detective with the Laramie Police Department. Although they'd solved a tough case, he'd rubbed her the wrong way the entire time.

Two words described him best. *Too much.* Too big. Too tall. Too broad. Too self-righteous. Too smart and shrewd to be a university campus cop.

Even his energy was too disquieting. His blue eyes too piercing. All that bundled in a package that was simply too handsome.

There was no denying the last part, no matter how hard she tried, but even thinking it made her skin prickle.

Matt Granger's perfect facade was infuriating.

Too good to be true. Everyone around him believed it was real. Not her. At fourteen, she'd learned that sometimes the devil pretended to be a saint. The pretense so convincing, so calculated, that even those closest couldn't see the evil lurking within.

"Yes, it's probably a disguise," Matt said. Wearing a black T-shirt that was too tight—the only reason he purchased that size was to show off his physique—blue jeans, badge clipped on his top, walkie-talkie hooked on his utility belt and a dark brown cowboy hat, he glanced down at her with one of those disapproving looks she'd grown to despise. "But it'll take some thought and maybe a day or two for him to change it. In the meantime, not only do we have his current disguise but also his MO. We'll make sure every student will be wary of anyone wearing an arm sling or a walking boot or even asking for physical assistance."

Something was better than nothing. Hannah nodded. "We should also encourage a buddy system of some sort."

"When I took over as campus police chief, there had been an uptick in thefts and sexual assault. So I helped the university form a student organization to promote safety. I'll call an emergency SAV meeting, and we can talk to them about it. They'll spread the word quickly."

"'SAV'?" she asked, vaguely remembering seeing a flyer with the acronym.

"Students Against Violence."

"Good idea—forming the organization and talking to them." Maybe he *was* making a difference on campus. Still didn't change the fact that he could make an even bigger one working for the LPD.

He flashed a wry grin. "Did you just pay me a compliment?"

Not on purpose. Her guard had slipped. She had a tendency to go soft around him and usually overcompensated for it by turning more surly than normal. "Don't let it go to your head. I'm undercaffeinated. I had expected a delicious flat white from your fancy, expensive-looking espresso machine when I showed up this morning." Clearly, his department had a healthy budget.

"Sorry about that. It's on the fritz. My office manager is working on getting it fixed."

She'd spotted Dennis Hill fiddling around with the machine. He hadn't really seemed like he knew what he was doing. Not that she was an expert in the handyman department.

"I'll buy you a cup of coffee in the cafeteria on the way out," he offered.

She needed a triple shot of espresso at this point, but if he was buying, then she'd even take the mediocre java from the hospital.

Matt took out his phone. "I better send Sergeant Starkey a text letting him know the sketch is on the way and what I want him to do with it."

The artist finished packing up his things and waved on his way out of the room.

Hannah went over to Jessica's bedside. "I know talking about all this is difficult, but it's important. We only have a few more questions for you." After Jessica nodded, Hannah proceeded. "Do you have a personal laptop?"

"Yeah. Of course."

"How often did you go to the computer lab?" Hannah asked.

Jessica pressed a palm to one of her bruised cheeks, resting her face in her hand. The bandage over her swollen nose—at least it wasn't broken—tugged at her pale skin. "Every Tuesday, Thursday and Saturday."

Matt stepped closer, coming up alongside Hannah. "Why only on those days?" he asked.

"I started going the first week of school. On the days when I have my engineering class—Tuesdays and Thursdays. I go on Saturdays now, too, to keep up with the workload."

Hannah made a note in her pad. "Why did you use the lab at all since you have a laptop?"

"Modeling software the university paid a license for is loaded on the computers in the lab. To use it on my personal laptop, I'd have to buy it. Costs a small fortune. Besides, my computer doesn't have the gigs to run it without the software glitching, anyway. The ones in the lab are a lot more powerful. And they offer free printing but don't advertise it. Those who know go there all the time just for that. I had planned to print out a paper for my Comm. 1 class." Tears welled in her eyes. "But I ran out of time because I wanted to catch the bus."

"You're slated to graduate next spring," Matt said. "Most

students take Communication 101 during their first year. Why did you wait so late?"

"I wanted to balance some of my more challenging coursework with easier classes. Thought it would be less stressful that way."

"Which one were you enrolled in?" Hannah asked. Comm. 1—as most students on campus called it—was offered twice that quarter: either Monday, Wednesday and Friday for an hour at three p.m. or Tuesday and Thursday for an hour and a half at nine a.m. The registrar's office was going to email a copy of Jessica's class schedule to Matt before noon, but the more ground they could cover now, the better.

"The one that's three days a week," Jessica said.

A chill slithered down Hannah's spine. They'd been in the same Comm. 1 class. Hannah didn't remember seeing Jessica, but the auditorium had been packed with students, many of them blond females.

"Besides the supposed bike accident, what else did you talk about before you were attacked?" Matt asked.

Jessica shrugged. "I don't know. Everything happened so fast. One second, he was helpless and nice. Kind of sweet. Like a wounded puppy. The next thing I knew, I felt the pinprick of the needle before I was even upright from the ground, and then he snatched the keys from my hand."

Victims sometimes had trouble recalling information, not wanting to relive the trauma of the assault. "We need you to try to remember anything else that he said or did that might help us." Hannah held her watery gaze, her heart breaking for the woman and all the others who had been killed. "Any detail, no matter how small or insignificant, could be the key to stopping him before he has a chance to go after someone else."

Jessica nodded miserably and closed her eyes. A moment later, she said, "He offered to pay me back for helping him."

"Pay you back how?" Matt asked.

"With coffee at the Wheatgrass Café."

Hannah and Matt exchanged a look. She turned back to Jessica. "Did you go to the Wheatgrass often?"

"I usually grabbed lunch there. Since it was a short walk from the quad, it was convenient." Jessica's eyes flew open. "There is something else. Last night, while I was talking to him, I recalled running into him once before. I mentioned it to him."

"Do you remember where?" Hannah asked. "And when?"

"Mythology 101. But what day?" She shrugged. "Honestly, I don't know. Maybe when we had the lecture about the Titans. Last week, Tuesday or Thursday. I can't say for certain. But the class was from four to five."

"Are you sure you were the one who remembered him and not the other way around?" Matt asked.

"Yeah. I'm positive. He claimed not to recognize me."

A blatant lie after stalking her for days, weeks—who knew for how long. "To get you to lower your guard," Hannah said, thinking out loud.

"It worked." Jessica closed her eyes again for a second, just long enough for a shudder to shake her. "That's when he introduced himself. Told me his name was Theodore Cowell."

An alias, surely, but Hannah wrote it down anyway. Once they dug into the name, it might lead to something if they got lucky. She turned the page in her notebook, quickly going over all the places the other victims frequented. "Did you ever use the Sweetwater Rec Center?"

The fitness center was popular among the students.

Those who took at least six credit hours a quarter received free membership.

"My first year. I took a tour and the HOPES class."

"'HOPES'?" Hannah asked. She'd seen a brochure about it but had been focused on other things.

"It stands for Healthy Options for the Prevention and Education of Substances," Matt said. "They teach students to make healthy choices."

"The class wasn't preachy or judgmental at all." Jessica rubbed her arms. "I learned a lot."

"Do you remember who gave you the tour or who led the class?" Hannah asked.

"It was the same person—Perry Slagle."

Hannah made a note. She remembered the guy. He had approached her, offering to give her a tour, but she had declined. Perhaps that had been a mistake. "How often did you go back to the rec center?"

"I go swimming once a week. Great pool. Nice facility. But I honestly use the rec center more to decompress. I make appointments a couple of times a week to use the relax-wellness pod or the massage chair."

"Appointments online?" Hannah asked, writing it all down.

"Sometimes. You can also go to the Athletic Training Room the same day to see if they have any openings. Other than that, I bike everywhere during the day to keep the pounds off. At night, I always used the Secure Ride shuttle. I heard it's supposed to be safer."

The service was separate from the normal school bus, which ran a preplanned route on campus. Secure Ride only operated on weekdays from six p.m. to two a.m. and all day on the weekends. Students could also use the Secure Ride app to be picked up or dropped off at any location within the town limits during those hours.

"It is safer and has cut down on the number of DUIs and alcohol-related accidents," Matt said. "My department highly advises all students to use the free service."

"How long has the university had the program?" Hannah asked.

Matt met her gaze. "About twenty years."

Hannah arched a brow at him with a knowing look. They needed to investigate the drivers. He nodded in silent agreement.

Jessica wrapped her arms around her midsection. "Do you really think the guy who attacked me is the University Killer?"

"Yes." Hannah gave a solemn nod. "We do."

"I can't believe I fell for his act." Jessica's shoulders sagged as tears fell from her eyes. "How could I be so stu—"

"Hey, don't do that to yourself," Matt said, cutting her off, his voice warm and soothing. "What happened wasn't your fault. This guy is a predator. A cold-blooded killer who preyed on your kindness."

Hannah recognized the guilt swimming in Jessica's glassy eyes. She knew better than most how easy it was to allow an encounter with darkness to snuff out your own light. "Is there anything else you can remember?"

"No." Jessica sniffled, and Matt handed her a tissue. "I'm sorry."

So was Hannah. "You should seek counseling on campus. Talking to someone about what you went through could help you heal and move forward."

Therapy had helped Hannah make sense of her past. Of discovering her father was a monster. But no amount of counseling had stopped her from building walls around her heart. Or had changed her mind that love was a game for the foolhardy.

Matt scrubbed a hand over his jaw with a distant look like he was thinking about something. Hannah made a mental note to follow up on it. He wasn't the type of partner to withhold information, but it could slip a person's mind to mention it.

"I'll have an officer posted outside your door twenty-four-seven until we catch this guy. We'll keep you safe," Matt said. He had assigned campus cops to stand guard in twelve-hour shifts, from nine to nine.

"Try to focus on rest and recovery." Hannah pressed one of her cards into Jessica's cold hand. "If you remember anything else, please give us a call."

On their way out, the assigned officer, who was seated in a chair beside the door to the room, jumped to his feet. Carl Farran.

"You don't have to get up every time I pass you," Matt said.

Farran stood ramrod straight at attention. "Yes, Chief."

Hannah and Matt made their way down the hall.

She slipped her notebook into her blazer's pocket. "I don't think it's a good idea to have him on guard duty until his DNA results come back officially clearing him."

"Duly noted," Matt snapped, and the know-it-all hotshot kept walking without a glance at her.

"That's it? You're not pulling him?"

"No. I am not." As she opened her mouth to protest, he raised a hand, silencing her. "When the first victim was murdered almost ten years ago, Carl was twelve and weighed ninety pounds soaking wet. I know that because I checked with his former pediatrician. Does that sound like the rapist and murderer of a grown woman? Or one with the knowledge to cover their tracks?"

She looked back at Officer Farran over her shoulder. He had sat down and was watching them walk to the elevator. Lanky and unassuming and baby faced, he didn't look like a twisted killer. But neither had her father. "No, it doesn't, but you're the one who likes to keep everything clean. Having a suspect, who hasn't been formally cleared guarding our witness is messy. Not to mention reckless." She'd been itching to throw that word back in his face. It had hurt when he'd called her that.

With anyone else, their insults and judgments didn't bother her. For some reason, only Matt got to her. She hated that he thought she wasn't good at her job and wasn't a smart detective.

"Label it what you want," he said, not looking the least bit fazed. "Carl is not a suspect. He's a person of interest at most, and even that is a stretch. I've got to use my people efficiently. In order to prevent this guy from snatching another woman, I need my most experienced officers patrolling campus. Not babysitting."

"You agreed to do this my way."

Stopping short, he pinned her with a stern look and nudged the brim of his cowboy hat up with a knuckle. "I did. And I will. But on this, don't push me. We've got plenty of reasons to fight. A common-sense decision shouldn't be one of them."

Matt was a stickler for the rules and playing things by the book. His motto was *No such thing as too careful*. This approach was out of character for him. Then again, she'd never seen him in charge of a team or a department with people to manage. Either way, she wasn't going to push this, since Farran was too tall—only a couple of inches shorter than Matt—to be the man she had encountered last night. The guy they were looking for was between five-ten and six-foot, possibly five-nine. Footwear could alter height an inch or two. "We need to see if there's surveillance footage of the Mythology 101 class."

"Not sure how much help it will be, since he was wearing his disguise, but I'll have Starkey look into it, along with a list of drivers working when Jessica and Madison Scott rode the Secure Ride," Matt said.

"Our perp mentioned the Wheatgrass Café for a reason. All ten victims frequented the place." She'd made an effort to swing by the café twice a day while undercover.

"Might just be because it's familiar to everyone on campus, but I think we should check it out, too. Let's grab coffee there instead of the cafeteria," he suggested.

"We also need to speak to the Comm. 1 professor," Hannah said. "Every victim took the same class."

"Right along with every other student. It's a prerequisite to graduate, regardless of your degree."

"Even more reason to talk to him."

"The only problem is that over the past nine years, the instructor has changed four different times. Other than the syllabus, the classes have nothing in common."

Frustration bubbled up in Hannah. "Great." Bye-bye to a possible lead.

"Except for one thing." Matt pressed the call button for the elevator. "The location."

"Go on," she said, gesturing for him to elaborate.

"The auditorium is right across the hall from where Dr. Bradford Foster has held his classes for the past eleven years. He teaches two popular courses. Psychology of Crime and Justice and Psychology of Serial Killers. That's not all—one of the victims from the last time the University Killer surfaced was a student of his."

"His field of expertise would enable him to know how to be a serial murderer without getting caught."

"My thoughts exactly."

The elevator chimed.

"When we were wrapping up with Jessica, you got that look in your eye," Hannah said.

"What look is that?"

The doors opened, and they stepped on.

"Like you found a piece to the puzzle."

He shook his head. "I wish. After that poor girl almost blamed herself for what happened, I thought about how different serial killers go after their victims."

Hannah hit the button for the lobby. "There's more to it than that." She could tell by his strained tone that he was filtering his ideas. "I hate it when you hold back." Only his thoughts. Not his criticism.

"It's nothing, really. A few nights ago, I streamed a movie about Ted Bundy. I was thinking specifically about him. The ruses he used to lure his victims to the vicinity of his vehicle. A plaster cast on a leg. A sling on one arm. Sometimes hobbled on crutches. Then he asked for assistance in carrying something to his vehicle. Our guy did practically the same thing. Almost as though he'd watched the movie and had taken notes."

"You're right." Hannah's mind churned over what Matt had said. "His MO is pretty similar." She took out her cell phone.

"What is it?" Matt asked.

"You might be on to something," she said, typing into the search engine. She hit Enter, pulled up the page she was looking for and scanned it. Two paragraphs down, she found it. "That son of gun." She turned her phone so Matt could see the page. "Ted Bundy was born *Theodore Robert Cowell*."

"The name he gave Jessica."

The elevator stopped, and the doors opened once more.

"This is some kind of game to him," she said, getting off the elevator with Matt. "He puts the queen of hearts playing card on the body of his victims." She kept her voice to a whisper as they headed for the outer doors. "He is bold enough to rape them without a condom, leaving behind his DNA."

"He's not afraid of getting caught. Brazen. Must be confident that he's not in any database."

"Not yet, anyway," Hannah agreed. "But the amount of bleach he used in the vehicle is a sure sign he didn't want to leave DNA there. On his victims is fine, but not in the car. Why?"

"Control, is my guess. The body he discards, while the car is his domain, a part of his hunting ground. He spends a lot of time in it and wants to keep it clean. Hence, the bleach."

She was impressed by his insight. "Makes sense." Further proof he was wearing the wrong badge. Working with him had been a challenge on multiple levels, but they had closed one of the toughest cases of her life. Maybe together they could do it again.

With a whoosh, the outer doors opened, and they stepped outside into the brisk morning air. She shivered against the crisp breeze and glanced at Matt's bare arms. "You're not chilly?"

"I run hot."

"Why does that not surprise me?" Everything about the guy was hot. Matt Granger definitely had raw physical appeal.

Shake it off, she mentally chided herself.

"You're one to talk," he said with a smug expression. "All I get from you is fire or ice."

She couldn't deny it and wouldn't apologize for it. "We all deal with stress differently." Even the stress of sexual tension, but her current source was about this case. "I feel like there's this clock in my chest, counting down to when our guy makes his next move." They only had twelve days left in the month for him to claim his next two victims. "He's been so slippery for so long." She was terrified of failing yet again.

"I bet he didn't plan on firing his gun. He only did it because you surprised him. It was a mistake. Ballistics will be back tomorrow. It might turn up something."

The murderer using the university as his hunting ground strangled his victims, which wasn't quick or easy. The act was personal and didn't leave ballistics traces.

Matt put his hand on her shoulder, giving it a light squeeze, and she found his touch reassuring even though she wished she didn't. "No matter what game this sicko is playing, we're going to make sure that in the end, he doesn't win."

Chapter Five

As Matt opened the door to the Wheatgrass Café, his cell phone buzzed. He took it out of his pocket and glanced at the caller ID. "It's Starkey," he said to Hannah. "Order me a large black coffee with two pumps of vanilla syrup."

She made a gagging face over the amount of sugar. "I thought you were buying."

He whisked out his wallet and tossed it to her. "What's up?" he said, answering the phone and walking away from the entrance.

"Flyers with the University Killer's likeness have been made and printed."

"You included the warning at the bottom in bold, red font?"

"I read the text you sent, Chief. It's done. The flyers are being put up all over campus as we speak, starting with the quad since it gets the most traffic. I sent a copy to the news station. It'll air within the hour and from there around the clock. I also emailed a copy to Erica Egan."

Matt's blood pressure spiked at hearing the name. "I don't want my department dealing with her. She only writes sensationalized articles with flagrant disregard for the feelings of innocent people." The woman had written stories that had wounded members of his family. Mostly his cousins Holden and Sawyer and his new wife, Liz. "My department doesn't do her favors. You got it?"

"Sorry. But we wanted a copy to go the *Laramie Gazette*, right?"

"To the *Gazette*. Not to Egan. Send it to the editor in chief next time."

"She slipped me her card one day and said if I had anything for the paper that it should go directly to her. What's the problem?"

Pinching the bridge of his nose, Matt shook his head over the sergeant's naivete. "Did she slip it to you one day or one night over drinks while she was cozying up to you in a bar?" Dead silence on the other end of the line was the only answer he needed. "May I remind you that you are a married man? With kids?" Granted, they weren't little, but even at eighteen and twenty, they'd feel the impact of an affair. "Don't mess up a good thing."

"I didn't go home with her. Only a little harmless flirting," Starkey said, but Matt knew there was nothing harmless about that viper. "She's nice."

Matt huffed out an annoyed breath. "And pretty. And sexy." The kind weak men found irresistible. "And willing to cross any line to break a story and see her name in the byline below the headlines. Stay away from her. Do we have an understanding?"

"Sure do. I'll get the flyers disseminated."

"Hold on. I need you to find out if there are any surveillance videos of the Mythology 101 class last week on Tuesday and Thursday. I want to know if there's any footage of our guy interacting with Jessica Atkinson. Also, get with transit services about the Secure Ride app. We need them to give us a list of drivers who picked up or dropped off both Atkinson and Scott."

"Roger that."

"Where's Dennis?" Matt asked, needing his office manager to handle something for him.

"He's still tinkering around with the espresso machine."

"I want him to call everyone on the SAV contact list and set up an emergency meeting at six o'clock in the lobby of the Student Union." Most of them would be done with their classes by that time, and the building was adjacent to the quad, making it easy to get to the dorms for those who lived there.

"I'll tell him."

"And I want of stack of flyers waiting for me there so I can pass them out at the meeting."

"We'll make it happen, Chief."

Matt disconnected, tucked his phone in his pocket and headed back inside the café. Hannah was at the counter with two large to-go cups and a couple of protein bars in front of her, notepad out, and talking to the manager, a woman in her fifties or sixties.

"Ma'am." He tipped his hat at the manager and read her name tag: Barbara S.

"This is my partner, Campus Police Chief Matt Granger," Hannah said.

"I'm aware." Barbara offered a pleasant smile. "The school paper did a wonderful piece on you. As I was telling Detective Delaney, you're looking at my usual crew. They work flex hours between them Monday through Friday, five a.m. to six p.m. I work at the register on the weekends. It's a lot slower when classes aren't in full swing. Other than that, they fill in when they can." She gestured to her staff.

Matt looked over at the workers. Four of them—two girls and two boys. They were barely twenty years old. One guy had braces, and the other—at two hundred pounds and five-five—didn't meet the physical description. "How long have they worked for you?"

"A couple of them since last year," Barbara said. "The other two are new hires that started right before the quarter began."

"Does anyone run deliveries for you?" Hannah asked.

"We only deliver to the university hospital and the campus police department. Otherwise, I'd need a dedicated runner. As it stands right now, I send one of them to make the deliveries and I handle the register while they're gone."

Matt picked up his cup and a protein bar. "Thank you for your time."

Sipping her coffee, Hannah strolled out of the café ahead of him. Her long blond hair was loose, swaying a bit as she walked and catching the late-day sunlight when she stepped outside.

On the sidewalk, he faced her. She wore a navy blazer over a fitted V-neck tee, jeans, booted heels, her badge clipped to her belt and her gun holstered on her hip. Even though she still had a dewy glow to her complexion and appeared younger than her age, without the ponytail, there was no hint of a girl. Standing in front of him, she looked formidable—all woman.

He held up the protein bar. "Is this supposed to be a power lunch?" he asked, wondering what happened to the woman who loved hearty meals.

"More like a power snack. I remember you need sustenance every couple of hours, or you get cranky. And trust me, I prefer it when you're not cranky." With a hint of a grin, she handed him his wallet. "I'm surprised you trusted me with it."

"Why?" He took the leather bifold and slipped it back in his pocket.

"Who simply hands over their wallet?"

"You're my partner, not a stranger. It's not as if you're going to steal my credit card number. Plus, I don't have anything to hide." He opened the protein bar and bit into it.

Tipping her head to the side, she studied him for a long moment.

"What is it?" he asked, her silent scrutiny making him uneasy.

"Nothing. Just trying to figure you out." She took a sip of coffee and put her bar in her pocket. "Peel beneath the *perfect* outer layers."

Perfect? The way she'd uttered the word didn't sound like a compliment, but he was the first to admit that he wasn't without flaws. "I could say the same."

A quirk of a smile played around one corner of her mouth. "If you want to know me, you're wasting your time. There's nothing more to me than this—a woman with a badge and a gun, determined to put the bad guys away no matter the cost to myself."

How grudgingly she let go of bits of herself. "Maybe that's all you *want* there to be, but there's more." *A lot more.* And he was going to do some peeling of his own.

"Believe what you want." She threw on a pair of sunglasses and looked away. "I say we speak to Slagle next."

"The Sweetwater Rec Center is only three blocks over," Matt said. "Want to walk and stretch our legs?"

"We may as well. I need to burn off some energy. Besides, the College of Arts and Sciences building is right across the quad from the fitness center."

Matt ate his protein bar and finished his coffee on the fifteen-minute walk. He chucked his trash in the waste receptacle near the front doors of the rec center. "Do you know what this guy looks like?"

"Buzz cut. Dark hair. Brown eyes. Clean shaven every time I've seen him." She opened the door, and he walked in behind her. "Lean and wiry. Easy to tell he works out a lot. A bit under six feet. Looks like he could be in his late thirties. Real chatty. I found it off-putting. And he's very enthusiastic."

The facility had been renovated and expanded a few years back. At twenty-thousand square feet, it was massive and state-of-the-art. If Matt had time to indulge, he'd use the equipment here, but plenty of work on the ranch kept him fit.

"Can I help you?"

He turned his attention to a woman sitting at the reception counter behind a stack of towels.

Hannah flashed her badge. "We need to speak with Perry Slagle. Is he around?"

The woman's smile faltered as she looked at the badge prominently displayed on Matt's shirt. "Sure." She picked up the phone and pressed a button. "Hi, Perry. The police are here to speak with you." She listened for a moment. "Okay. I'll let them know." Hanging up, she glanced at them. "He's about to get someone set up in the CryoLounge Recovery Chair. He'll come out front as soon as he's done."

"Will he? How nice of him," Hannah said. "Where can we find him?"

"In the Wellness Room." She pointed over her shoulder. "Back through there."

Hannah stalked off like she knew where to go.

Matt trailed along, his gaze darting around. Glass, mirrors, sleek equipment and sweaty bodies as far as the eye could see.

They passed a large sign that read *Wellness Room*. It didn't take them long to find Perry standing beside a student the size of football player, who was reclining in what appeared to be a comfortable space-age lounge chair.

"I've got it programed to gradually decrease the temperature since it's your first time, buddy. But trust me," Perry said, talking a mile a minute, "you're going to feel incredible afterward and even better over the next few days. Say goodbye to muscle fatigue. This is just as effective as an ice bath, without the inconvenience of getting wet."

Hannah sighed. "What did I tell you?"

"Maybe he'll talk himself into a confession."

"Perry Slagle," Hannah said, and the guy turned toward her. She held up her badge. "We need a word with you."

"After thirty minutes, you'll be good to go." Perry patted the student on the shoulder. He came over to them with a pleasant smile, his eyes bright and sparkling with energy. "I told Mindy I'd be out front in a sec." No hint of an attitude in his friendly tone.

"We didn't feel like waiting," Hannah said, guiding him out into the hall.

"What can I do for you?" Squinting, he stared at Hannah. "I know you. You refused to take a tour last week. Didn't even want to see the fifty-two-foot rock wall. Everyone wants to take a gander at that thing, even if they don't ever climb it. I thought you were a student."

"I'm Detective Delaney. This is Campus Police Chief Granger. We're investigating the murder of a student, Madison Scott."

"Oh yeah. I read about that in the *Laramie Gazette*. So sad."

"Did you know her?" Matt asked.

"We weren't friends, if that's what you mean, but I remember her. Talking to her. Seeing her here."

Hannah took out her notepad. "Did you happen to give her a tour?"

Perry shrugged. "I don't know. It's possible. We don't keep records of tours, but I give them all the time. I love getting people excited about the facility and fitness."

"Do you know if she took your HOPES class?" Matt asked.

"As a matter of fact, she did. Last month. Sweet girl. She also brought along her roommate. I encourage the more, the merrier for my HOPES class. Unlike some substance abuse–prevention programs that rely on a fear-based approach and promote a *just say no* message, HOPES takes a more positive approach and focuses on harm reduction. I recognize that college students are young adults, who have the intellectual capacity to make responsible, informed decisions about their substance use. Heck, I've an eighteen-year-old enrolled here myself."

Hannah looked up from her notes. "Do you keep records of who attends those classes?"

"We have to. The class is mandatory for all first-year students, as well as those who transfer in with less than sixty credits and those who are twenty-one years of age and younger."

Matt and Hannah exchanged a quick glance. That would've been every victim.

"The gym is open from five in the morning until ten at night," Matt said. "What's your work schedule?"

"I'm usually here during the weekday from nine to three, but I also do personal training outside of those hours. I'm off on weekends, unless I have a one-on-one class."

"Must be nice to have such a flexible schedule," Hannah said.

Grinning, Perry folded his arms, his T-shirt exposing rock-solid biceps and powerful forearms. "My wife certainly appreciates it. She's a nurse at the university hospital. Works nights. I pick up the slack with the kids. And when Tina is off, I get extra me-time."

"'Kids'?" Matt asked. "You only mentioned you have a kid going to SWU."

"He was our surprise baby when we were seniors here ourselves. We decided to wait to have more. Our other son is twelve and our daughter is ten."

Three kids. Sounded stressful. "Where were you eleven nights ago, on Saturday the seventh, between twelve thirty and one thirty in the morning?"

They didn't know the precise time Madison Scott had been taken, but they did have a time of death.

Perry's gaze darted around as he thought about it. "That was Labor Day weekend. My wife took the younger ones to Boise to visit her parents. On Saturday, I was home, watching the football game. SWU versus Las Vegas. Started at eight forty-five. Didn't end until almost one in the morning. Went into overtime. Good game. Our star quarterback, Linder, is going to be a first- or second-round draft pick— mark my words."

"Did you watch the game alone?" Matt asked.

"Yeah."

Hannah finished writing. "Where were you last night between ten and eleven p.m.?"

"I was home with the kids. My wife was at work."

"What time do they go to bed?" Matt asked.

"Eight thirty, if they've got school the next day. Otherwise, ten."

"Are your children good sleepers?" Matt gave an easy smile to keep the guy from getting guarded. "Any trouble with them getting up in the middle of the night asking for water? Nightmares? That sort of thing?"

"I'm lucky. I've got sound sleepers. I cut off liquids one hour before bed. And don't tell my wife, but if one is acting restless or cranky, I give them a kiddie sleep gummy."

No alibi for Scott's murder, and he could've easily snuck out last night while his kids had been asleep. Now for the hard part. "Would you consent to giving us a DNA sample?"

Perry's smile fell. "Why? I'm not a suspect, am I?"

"We're looking at common connections between the victims," Hannah said, "and you happen to be one of them. The sample would take thirty seconds. A buccal swab. We brush a Q-tip on the inside of your cheek. That's it. Then we can cross you off our list."

Perry nodded, unease glinting in his eyes, his jaw tightening. "Yeah, yeah. That makes sense. But kind of sounds invasive, too."

"It would be really helpful," Matt added.

"I want to help. I do. I've got nothing to hide, but I still don't see how I figure into the equation."

"Of course you don't, and the sooner we don't have to look in your direction, the better for everyone. How about you come by the station after work today?" Matt asked. "It'll only take a second. I promise."

"I can't." Perry lowered his head, his gaze shifting around. "Today isn't good." He looked up at them. "I think I might want to talk to my wife and a, um, a lawyer first. Is that okay with you?"

They'd lost him. He would never voluntarily give a DNA sample after speaking with a lawyer.

Hannah stiffened, probably sensing the same. "Sure."

"Am I free to go now?" Perry asked.

Matt nodded. "You are. If we have any additional questions, we know how to find you."

Perry hurried away down the hall, not glancing back at them.

"All the victims have the HOPES class in common. They have *him* in common." Hannah pointed at Perry.

"Not to mention he had opportunity with Scott and Atkinson." It was difficult to ask people to recall where they were two to three years ago, much less nine.

"Maybe we give him a couple of days to squirm. To worry. I doubt he'll talk to a lawyer and certainly not his wife. Raising the subject with her could cause marital strife. Then, when he doesn't think we're still looking at him, we speak to him again. Lean harder—and next time we'll bring the buccal-swab kit with us."

"Let's go talk to Dr. Foster." Matt turned for the entrance. "We might have better luck with him."

Chapter Six

At the College of Arts and Sciences building, Dr. Foster's class was still in session.

"What time does it end?" Hannah asked, staring at one of the SWUPD flyers that had already been taped on the wall.

Along with the drawing of the suspected University Killer was other pertinent information: Male. White. Approximate height. Medium build. His use of medical devices and request for assistance as a ploy. The vehicle driven, a dark SUV—possibly a Chevy Tahoe or GMC Yukon, after she had reviewed plenty of makes and models and had narrowed it down.

At the bottom, in bold, red text, was a warning:

Be advised that the suspect is most likely wearing a disguise and his physical appearance may change. Stay alert. Use the buddy system.

"Two thirty," Matt said.

Hannah glanced at her watch. They'd have to wait forty-five minutes.

She spun around and faced the large auditorium doors across the hall. "His class ends right before Comm. 1 begins. He could easily watch students flowing into the room. It's usually packed. I'd say two hundred, maybe more. Fifty-three percent of the student body is female." Hannah fished out her notebook and flipped through the pages. "The Mythology 101 class that Jessica took was Tuesday and Thursday at four p.m. Do you know if Dr. Foster has a class at that time?"

"Easy enough to look up." He grabbed his phone and did a quick search of Foster's classes. "He doesn't teach on those two days this quarter."

Pivoting on her heel, she eyed the doors to Foster's room. There were two ways to approach it. Wait until the doctor was finished with his class and then catch him off-guard. If they went in now, they'd lose the element of surprise—but by the same token, their presence might rattle him. "Why don't we sit in and listen to his lecture? We might learn something."

"It's your call."

On the walk over, to keep the chitchat with Matt to a minimum, she'd read the professor's bio, getting up to speed on him. Divorced. Two kids. Both attended SWU. He'd written a couple of books, worked as a consultant for the Seattle Police Department before he relocated from Washington to Wyoming. Now she was ready to see him in action.

She pulled the door open and crept inside. Matt followed behind her into the dimly lit room. Unlike the auditorium across the hall, this one was much smaller, seating fewer than fifty.

Dr. Bradford Foster was at the front of the room, standing before his presentation as he clicked on to the next slide.

His gaze flickered up to Hannah and Matt as they found seats in the top back row.

"The making of a serial killer is never clear, and every case won't fit inside the same box," the professor said. "Many factors can lead a person to become a violent adult, from causality to mental illness. There is so much variation between each serial murderer, one cannot generalize them beyond the simple definition that they have killed at least two victims with a cooling-off period between those murders, ranging from hours to years. With that being said, there tends to be common characteristics that can be found in the psychopath personality disorder. Lack of remorse and empathy. A strong impulsivity. The need for control." Foster walked around the front of the room, using lots of hand gestures. "Not every psychopath is a serial killer, but rather, various serial murderers present some psychopathic traits. A charming personality. Pathological liar. Like to think of themselves as all-knowing. Have great self-esteem but also some antisocial traits." He brought up the next slide. "Now, let's look at causality before we dive into today's notorious killer."

The students were absorbed in his lecture, their gazes following his every movement more than looking at the slides. Most seemed to be recording the class on their phones and laptops rather than taking copious notes.

Hannah had to hand it to him—Dr. Foster was an engaging orator. He had a fluid way of dissecting the minds of psychopathic killers, identifying their uncontrollable urges, anger, excitement or the need for attention as the drive for the offender's behavior. His style lessened the danger and with that, the degree of fear one should have regarding a brutal monster.

"I like to alternate between examining serial killers of

the past with those more recently brought to light. Last time, we looked at Jack the Ripper. Today, Edward Ressler."

Hannah stiffened in her seat, her blood going cold.

Dr. Foster clicked onto another slide, bringing up a picture of her father. Suddenly, it was like all the air had been sucked out of the room and she couldn't breathe.

Matt leaned over, bringing his mouth close to her ear, putting a gentle hand on her forearm. "Are you all right?"

Frozen, she couldn't immediately respond. Matt must have sensed or seen her distress but didn't know the cause. No one knew Hannah's real identity, that she was Anna Ressler, the daughter of a serial killer. Not even Matt.

She stared straight ahead at the image on the screen, right into the familiar dark eyes, and nodded.

"Sure?" he whispered, the concern in his voice tugging at her heart.

Hannah cleared her throat. "Yeah. Fine." She was anything but fine. She wanted to run from the eighteen-by-twenty-four picture enlarged on the screen, out the auditorium, through the front doors of the building and keep going until she forgot she was the spawn of pure evil.

"Even though he targeted mostly women in his county in Colorado, he was known as the Neighborhood Killer. He tortured and murdered more than forty people," Foster said, a burning ache building in Hannah's chest. "Ressler was known as an upstanding pillar of his community, who attended church weekly. A good husband. A devoted father."

Hot bile rose in her throat. It was all true. Before he was caught, her childhood memories had been fond ones. Standing on his toes and twirling around in the living room, listening to folk-rock music. Hiking in the Rocky Mountains. Church on Sundays. Weekend fishing trips. Grilling in the backyard.

Heart-wrenching images flooded her, and she struggled to push them away. She tightened her hands into fists, her nails digging into her palms.

"His wife, Mary-Beth, was married to him for twenty years and claimed she never suspected a thing. After he was arrested, he later admitted that when he got married, he stopped killing for a while—that cooling-off period—because of his wife. He was able to bury his alter ego. You might be asking yourselves, *Then what happened to make him start up again?*" A dramatic pause for effect. "He became a father," Dr. Foster said with a chuckle.

Some of the students laughed along with him.

But the words were a blistering hot knife in Hannah's chest. She'd heard it all before, but each time, the emotional wound reopened as though it had never healed.

"Ressler claimed the stressors of parenthood drove him to release his rage and thirst for blood once again," the professor said. "Ironically, it was his daughter, Anna, who led to his capture and arrest."

Sweat rolled down Hannah's spine. Her heart raced with dread. To have her father, her life—*her misery*—dissected like a lab rat, the intestines picked at and examined under a microscope as a lesson for these kids who had no concept of what it meant to live with and love someone truly evil.

Finding it hard to breathe, she pressed her fingertips to the base of her throat. Her pulse thrummed under her skin. Unwelcome fears of betrayal and loss tangled together and curled around her chest like choking vines.

Dr. Foster pivoted and glanced at the clock on the wall. "Okay, guys, we're going to stop here today because we're out of time."

The class groaned in unison while Hannah exhaled a breath of relief.

Foster went to the wall and turned on the bright lights. Hannah squinted against the harsh glare. Students began packing up their things.

"Are you sure you're okay?" Matt asked, putting a palm on her knee. "You're pale as death. Look like you've seen a ghost."

What were the odds that Foster would lecture on her father today?

Hannah unclenched her hands. "I'm nauseous." That was putting it mildly. She wanted to puke. "Probably just low blood sugar." Another lie.

"Well, that's because you didn't eat that four-course lunch you bought us with my money," he said, joking about the protein bar. "You want to eat before we talk to Foster?"

Unable to stomach anything, she shook her head. Better to get this over with and then get some fresh air. "Come on." She gave his shoulder a tap, got up and headed down the stairs, passing the students filing out.

Once she reached the bottom of the stairs, a thought filled her with dread. What if Foster recognized her? Who she really was? Anna Ressler, spawn of the Neighborhood Killer.

The pictures of her in the media were of a fourteen-year-old girl. Surely Foster had refreshed his memory, going over everything about her father before the lecture.

She slowed, letting Matt walk ahead of her.

Matt gave her another concerned glance before approaching the professor. "Excuse me, Dr. Foster, we'd like a word with you. I'm Campus Police Chief Matt Granger, and this is my partner, Detective Hannah Delaney."

She would've preferred it if Matt hadn't mentioned her first name, even if it had been slightly changed. She went by her mother's maiden name, and *Hannah* was close enough to *Anna* for Foster to piece it together if she looked familiar to him.

Searching Foster's eyes for a reaction to her name, she spotted a flash of recognition, but then it was gone. It must've been nothing.

"Good afternoon, Officers." Bradford Foster switched off the projector. "What can I do for you?"

The professor stood around five feet, ten inches tall and, for a man of fifty-two, was extraordinarily fit. His polo shirt hugged firm biceps and a trim waist. He had a full head of thick hair feathered with gray. His smile was gleaming white and friendly, his teeth straight.

"We'd like to speak to you about the resurgence of the University Killer," Matt said.

"Really?" Foster grabbed a blazer hanging on the back of his chair and pulled it on. "Would you like to take a look at the case and consult? I did a little freelance work for law enforcement in Seattle before I took the job here. They found my insight invaluable."

Another wave of nausea swamped her, and she put a hand on the side of the desk to steady herself. "We're aware of your freelance work—but no, that's not why we're here."

"Then what is it?" Foster asked, his face tanned and glowing like he invested in good skincare products.

Hannah took out her notepad. "Did you know Madison Scott?"

A slight frown crossed his face. "The young lady who was murdered a few days ago? No, certainly not."

"She took the Comm. 1 course right across the hall from this room," Matt said. "You may have seen her in passing, in between your classes. May have even spoken to her."

Foster straightened. "If so, I don't recall."

Matt reminded him of the date of her death. "Where were you that night between two and four a.m.?"

"I was home. Asleep. Alone," Foster said in an arrogant tone, like it was a challenge.

"Did you know Isabel Coughlin?" Matt asked.

Isabel had been the University Killer's last victim almost three years ago. Thirty months, to be precise.

Foster considered the question. "The name rings a bell."

"It should," Matt said. "She was one of your students before she was murdered. You gave her a C in this course."

"I can't remember everyone. Perhaps she should have paid closer attention to my lectures." Foster closed his laptop and tucked it inside his leather messenger bag. "I do my best to empower my students with the tools necessary to spot psychopathic tendencies and avoid danger."

Hannah tightened her grip on her notepad at his callous tone.

Matt mentioned the day and time of Isabel Coughlin's death. "Do you recall your whereabouts?"

"I do not. It was a long time ago."

She hadn't bothered to jot down any notes because she could tell how this would go. "What about last night? Where were you between ten thirty and eleven?"

"Why? Was another woman abducted or attacked? If you let me take a look at the case file, I'm sure I could be of help."

Matt pulled on a tight grin. "Just answer the question. Where were you?"

"Home. Watching TV."

"Alone?" Hannah asked.

"As a matter of fact, yes." His confidence didn't waver for a second.

Hannah put her notepad away. "What were you watching?"

"A cooking show." Foster flashed a self-assured grin. "I think I'll try making the beef Wellington with truffle mashed potatoes and pairing it with a nice Bordeaux. More than enough for three. I could have you two over, and we could discuss the case like colleagues while I give you input."

A hard pass on dinner with this smooth talker. She wasn't sure she'd be able to stomach a meal with him.

Matt stepped closer, invading his personal space just a bit. "What vehicles do you own?"

"I drive a light blue BMW Z4. Why?"

Winters in Wyoming must be tough for the professor with a Z4. Next to impossible to drive through more than five inches of snow. Accumulations of ten to fifteen inches or more for a single storm weren't uncommon. Most people around there who had a little sports car also had a second vehicle, something a bit more rugged.

"Would you consent to DNA testing?" she asked. "Simply to rule you out so we can move on to real suspects."

"I think not." Foster picked up his messenger bag and slung the strap on his shoulder. "The idea of my DNA sitting in a database makes me uneasy."

She bet it did, but she also reminded herself that even innocent people were cautious.

"How about letting us take a look at your vehicle and where you keep it?" Matt suggested. "I'm sure it's a beauty and you like to park it in the garage."

The point was to get in the door with consent and then push the boundaries of their exploration a bit to see what they might find.

Foster chuckled, showing his pearly whites. The smile

was more feral than friendly. "How about you get a warrant, and then you can take a look?"

Hannah heard the bitter defensiveness in his tone and knew then that it was time to pivot.

The professor brushed past them, going toward the stairs.

"We didn't mean to offend you," Hannah said, starting after him. "We're just following procedure." He kept walking. "On second thought, discussing the case over some wine and beef Wellington sounds like a good idea."

She still didn't want to break bread with the man, but the idea of having access to his home and getting a sample of his DNA was appealing.

Foster stopped on the steps and turned around slowly. "So one of you can tiptoe off to my bathroom, find my comb and put some of my hair in an evidence bag? Or pocket a fork I used?" He shook his head. "Do you take me for a fool, Detective Delaney? The opportunity to graciously accept my assistance is gone."

Matt came up alongside Hannah. "Only a guilty person or someone with something to hide wouldn't cooperate with us," he said.

"Au contraire. If a person is innocent, there is no obligation to prove it to the police. Every smart citizen should take this approach. Trying to convince the authorities to reverse their suspicions only exposes a person to considerable risk with little to no benefit. It's one of the things I teach in my Psychology of Crime and Justice course. You two should enroll. I guarantee you'd both learn plenty."

Hannah stepped closer to Foster, drawing his smug gaze. "You don't have an alibi. Probably because of your antisocial traits despite your great self-esteem. Charming?" She didn't think he was, but his students seemed to. "Check. All-knowing? Check—at least, *you* think you are. Need for control? Check." She didn't mention *pathological liar*, but given enough time with him she could probably check that one off, too.

They stared at each other until his face turned from cocksure to uncomfortable.

"My students love my charm and wit, and my controlled nature has served me well," Foster countered. "I see no reason to apologize for being an expert in my field. Yes, apparently, I knew one of the victims, and another took a class across the hall from where I teach around the same time."

"All the victims took a class across the hall from where you teach," Matt said.

Foster didn't bat an eyelash. "Coincidence. Nothing more. Yes, I have no alibi for Madison Scott's murder or for whatever related incident might have happened last night that you're also investigating. But what about motive? Let's say for argument's sake that I am the University Killer. What would have angered me or enticed me to kill after all this time?"

Another challenge. Testing them.

"Last month, you were passed over for tenure," Matt said. "I heard you didn't take it well."

Foster's expression went deadpan.

Hannah gave him a small smile. "Sounds like a motive to me."

"I'm an esteemed professor and was given assurances that I'd make tenure next time. If that's all you've got, let's see how you two fare getting a warrant." Foster took a couple more steps, stopped again and looked back at them. "You local cops, regardless of what city or small hick town, are all the same," he said with disdain. "Never recognizing when you're out of your depth, outmatched and outsmarted. Or when you could use assistance from an expert. Not working with me is your loss. But let me give you a piece of advice, not that your egos will allow you to take it—you could use help from a profiler. Otherwise, he's going to kill two more women and then go quiet again for a few more years. And when he does, you'll wish you had accepted my initial proposal for me to provide input." He hurried up the steps and out of the auditorium.

Matt folded his arms and leaned back against a chair. "What's your assessment of him?"

"Even if he's not the University Killer, I don't like him. He has this air of superiority. Too controlled, with that all-knowing smugness, which, by the way, are characteristics of a serial killer that he listed."

"Agreed."

"And the last bit about recommending we use a profiler felt twisted. Like he was using reverse psychology. Make us feel inadequate so we double down and prove that we can catch this guy without any outside assistance." *I see you, Bradford Foster—and your little mind games.*

If only they had a profiler on the Laramie PD. She'd go straight to them with the case file.

"Agreed," Matt said again.

She looked at him in disbelief. "Come on, you've got to have more thoughts than that. I can see it on your face that you do."

"Am I that easy to read, or have you made studying me your hobby?"

He wasn't easy to read. Not one little bit. "Your thoughts?"

"I think since he lives on campus, I'm going to have an officer tail him in plainclothes. May as well rifle through his trash while we're at it and get a sample of his DNA to be on the safe side."

Sometimes there were moments, such as this one, when

they were in perfect sync instead of in opposition, and she wanted to give him something more affectionate than a high five or fist bump.

"I also think that, reverse psychology or not, the professor was right." Matt took out his cell phone. "We need a profiler."

Once again, they were of like mind. "You say that while you're dialing as though you have one in your contacts list."

By way of admission, he smiled and gave a small shrug.

This man never ceased to amaze her.

Chapter Seven

"Thanks, Liz. You're the best. Tell Sawyer I'm looking forward to seeing you guys at Thanksgiving." Matt hit the disconnect button and met Hannah at the top of the steps in the auditorium.

While he was on the phone, she had done laps around the room, going up and down the steps countless times. The woman had boundless energy. But he'd noticed she still hadn't eaten.

"Well?" she asked him as they pushed out the doors into the corridor.

"Success."

Once they got outside the building, he explained. "My cousin, Sawyer Powell—"

"One of the four cousins you live with out on the Shooting Star Ranch?"

"Sort of, kind of." That had come out of left field. "Anyway, Sawyer recently married Liz Kelley."

"The famous FBI agent who was out here helping him investigate?"

Sawyer and Liz had been in the news almost every day during their investigation "The very same."

"She profiles serial killers?" Hannah asked.

"No. Would you listen?"

They strolled across the quad, headed back to his car.

"Sorry. My mind is racing a mile a minute. I thought doing stairs while you were on the phone would help, but it hasn't."

He understood that problem. Working until you were bone-tired—as a police chief and on the ranch—solved that issue for him. "Eating might help," he suggested, but she shook her head. Something was still off with her. "Sawyer and Liz are out in Virginia. She works at Quantico."

"Home of the profilers. She called in a favor for you." Hannah glanced at him. "Oh, sorry. Please continue."

"That's it exactly. She put me on hold while she squared it all away. Nancy Tomlinson has agreed to look at our case file because of the urgency of the situation since we know our guy is going to try and kill two more women soon. We just need to send her what we have and keep her apprised of all updates. No matter how small."

Hannah raised her palm and waited for a high five.

So help him, he wanted to wrap her in a big hug and give her a kiss. Instead, he gave her a high five.

"Okay, now elaborate on the *sort of, kind of* part," she said, and he gave her a puzzled look, wondering what she was talking about. "Your living situation. I'll admit, I've been curious since we worked together."

Curious about where he sleeps? "We don't all live under one roof. My aunt and uncle live in the main house. Logan moved into the apartment above the garage once Sawyer moved out. Holden lives with his wife in a house his parents built for them on the property. Monty also lives in a house on the ranch, but alone."

She quirked an eyebrow. "Also built for him?"

"Yep."

"What about your parents?"

Where were all these rapid-fire questions suddenly coming from?

The last time they'd worked together, she wanted to know as little as possible about him. "My dad lives in the bunkhouse. My mom…" He shrugged, annoyed. Not at Hannah. At the topic of the woman who had abandoned her family. Abandoned him.

"And you?" she asked, not pressing the matter of his mother.

Talking about himself was never easy. Talking about himself in regard to his family was, well…tricky. "The majority of the ranch will be passed down to whichever Powell son decides to run the place. But my aunt Holly wanted me to have something." To assuage her guilt. Although she had nothing to feel guilty about. The person responsible for the harm done to him and his father was his mother, Holly's twin sister. "They let me pick a parcel of land, a couple thousand acres, where I built my own house." Put his sweat and blood into that place.

"What?" Hannah stopped in her tracks. "How big is the ranch?"

"Sixty."

"Sixty thousand acres?" she said slowly, in an astonished voice.

He nodded with a grimace because he knew what was coming next. "And no, I'm not rich. Holly and Buck Powell are. Yes, I accepted the land they gave me." Albeit located as far from the rest of the clan as he could get, almost living in Bison Ridge. And only to stop his aunt from blaming herself for the pain and suffering he'd experienced as a child. "But I am paying for it." In more ways than one. "I'm creating another source of revenue for the ranch on the land."

"For the Shooting Star Ranch, on *your* land?"

Matt's jaw tightened. "It's complicated."

Her eyes were serious yet soft as she studied him. This time, it didn't make him uneasy. "This is your thing, isn't it? We've all got one. A soft underbelly. This is yours."

She was exactly right. His family, his mother, his relationship with the Powells—it was indeed his soft spot. His weakness. And his strength.

Alarm bells went off in his head. She'd been acting strange since Foster's lecture, and after they'd questioned the professor, she'd only gotten worse. Nonstop moving. Not eating. The sudden interest in him, asking a ton of questions about his living situation of all things.

Deflecting from herself.

"What's your thing?" he asked.

She rocked back on her heels, her body tensing.

"Come on, Hannah. Tit for tat."

"It's the same as yours," she said grimly. "Family."

He frowned at her honest answer, which didn't tell him anything more than he already knew.

His cell chimed in his pocket. He took it out and read the text message from Starkey.

Transit wants you to swing by to discuss your request in person.

"What is it?" Hannah asked, in that frosty, distant way of hers, putting the wall back up between them.

Matt sighed bitterly, his elation over getting help from a profiler now gone. "We need to go to Transit Services to get the names of the Secure Ride drivers."

"Then what are we waiting for?"

IN THE LOBBY of the Transit Services center, Hannah hung back while Matt strode up to the front desk.

He introduced himself. "I'm here to speak with someone about an official request for information my department made earlier today."

The person at the front desk nodded and picked up the phone. Matt glanced over his shoulder at her, sporting an inquisitive expression, but she averted her gaze.

Hannah had gone from firing a fusillade of questions at him to being brusque, all in a sloppy effort not to overshare.

Foster's lecture had left her on edge and raw, and combined with Matt's uncanny way of getting her to lower her guard—simply by being himself—she was in danger of spilling secrets she'd kept half her life.

A man with rosy cheeks and a receding hairline, wearing glasses, left one of the back offices and came into the lobby. "I'm Otis Ortiz, the supervisor."

Matt shook his hand. "Chief Granger, and this is Detective Delaney."

Now he omitted her first name.

Sweat beaded Otis's forehead and upper lip. "I received your request for information, and I wish I could be of help, but we have a policy not to give out information about our employees."

"We're investigating the murder of Madison Scott and the attempted abduction of another student last night. The information I requested is vital. I'm sure if you fully understood the gravity of the situation, you wouldn't deny the request and subsequently obstruct justice."

Otis glanced around the lobby and met the prying gazes of the employees seated behind the front desk. "Why don't you come on back into my office?" Spinning on his heel, he hurried down the hall.

Matt and Hannah followed him into the office.

"Close the door," Otis whispered, and Hannah shut it. "Sit down."

Exchanging a glance, they both took seats, facing the desk.

"I already have the information you wanted printed, but I had to make a big show out there of not complying."

"Why is that?" Hannah asked.

Otis wiped his forehead with the back of his hand. "I'm in good health and I want to stay that way."

Matt's brow furrowed. "I don't understand. Care to explain?"

"Oh yeah, I was getting to that," Otis said in an exasperated way. "I cross-referenced the times Madison Scott and Jessica Atkinson used the Secure Ride with our drivers. Two names came up." Otis picked up a couple sheets of paper. "Bobby Evers and Shane Yates. Bobby has been in the hospital for the past four days. Since you mentioned an attempted abduction last night, I take it you probably don't still want his information."

"Why is he in the hospital?" Hannah asked.

"Appendicitis. They had to operate. He should be out in a day or two."

"Then you suppose right that we won't need his information," Matt said. "But that still doesn't explain your little act in the lobby."

"Yes, yes." Otis took a deep, shaky breath. "That brings me to the second driver and the reason for my ruse. Shane Yates," he said in a whisper.

"Is he here?" Hannah asked. "Are you afraid he'll overhear you speaking about him?"

"He's not in right now. Shane was supposed to work tonight, but he called in sick again. He does that whenever he feels like it."

Irritation ticked through Hannah. She pushed for a clear explanation. "Then why are you whispering?"

"I don't want any of the other employees to hear and then run back to him, saying I was a snitch."

Matt heaved a sigh, undoubtedly annoyed as well. "And you're afraid of him because…"

Otis stared at them like the answer was obvious. "Because snitches get stitches."

"If he's threatened or assaulted you in some way," Matt said, "we can write up a report, and it would be grounds for dismissal."

Pushing his glasses up the bridge of his nose, Otis shook his head. "I can't do that."

Matt took off his hat and ran a hand through his hair. "Why not?"

"Shane is with the biker gang."

Hannah pinned him with a glare, wishing he would simply tell them what they needed to know. "The Iron Warriors?"

That didn't sound like something their leader, Rip Lockwood, would allow. The guy was prior military and kept a tight leash on his men. He never made trouble for law enforcement. A tough guy for sure and undeniably hot if one was drawn to an edgy, bad boy on a motorcycle, but from what she knew of him, he didn't permit harassment and intimidation.

"If only." Otis shook his head. "I know Rip, the president of the Iron Warriors. We went to high school together. He even served in the Marines for a while. Good guy. Decent. He finally cleaned up the club, though it caused a big rift. All the guys doing illegal stuff broke off and formed a new club under Todd Burk. The Hellhounds."

Other than Todd Burk being a scumbag, the rest was news to Hannah. "When did this happen?"

"Last month."

"They've kept it pretty quiet," Matt said, clearly uninformed as well.

"They don't want to draw any unwanted attention." But Hannah was surprised she hadn't seen any new biker cuts around. Maybe she'd been too busy to notice.

"Where does the new gang hang out?" Matt asked.

Otis sat back in his chair with a grim expression. "Rip gave them the clubhouse of the Iron Warriors."

Whoa. The clubhouse was a single-story building that took up almost half the length of a city block. Rumor had it that every member had his own bedroom there so when they partied, they each had a private place to crash. It was her understanding that they had a bar, game room, armory, conference room, gym and dance area, complete with stripper poles. Handing over control of the facility was no small matter. "Why on earth would he do that?"

"To prevent bloodshed, I guess." Otis shrugged. "Todd didn't want to form a new club, and he didn't want to abide by Rip's rules," Otis said. "A lot of threats were made. Rip gave the Hellhounds the clubhouse to make the transition a peaceful one from what I've heard."

"And you're afraid to report or fire Shane because you think the Hellhounds will cause trouble for you if you do?" Hannah asked.

"Heck yeah, I'm afraid. And I don't *think*. I *know* they will."

"Then we'd bring them in," Matt said. "You'd press charges, and we'd put them away."

Otis flattened his lips into a grim line. "They would send a couple of prospects looking to earn their patches, wearing hoods, to bust the windows of my house and harass me. Even if you did catch them, the Hellhounds would make the next punishment even worse. It's just easier to keep Shane, not let anyone know I snitched and spare myself the misery."

"Give us his home address," Matt said.

Otis handed them the paper he was holding. Not only did it have Shane's address but also his schedule and his picture at the top of the page.

"Yates didn't work last night," Matt murmured.

Hannah stood. "If anyone asks whether you gave us any information, simply tell them you were forced to comply with a court order, and you'll be fine."

Otis's demeanor told her he was unconvinced. "For my sake, I hope so."

Matt took out a business card and grabbed a pen. "I'm giving you my personal cell number." He scrawled on the back of the card. "Call me day or night if you get any blowback on this." Putting his hat on, he stood and walked over to the door. "Thank you for your assistance."

They left the office and strode toward the lobby. Matt handed her the sheet on Shane Yates. She folded it and put it in her pocket.

One of the employees behind the desk eyed them as they pushed through the double doors, exiting the transit center. She looked over her shoulder and spotted the guy picking up the phone, his stare still glued to them.

"It's a good thing we drove over here," she said, headed for his campus police SUV.

"Why is that?"

"Because I have a sneaking suspicion that if we have any chance of catching Yates at home, we'll need to hurry."

Chapter Eight

As Matt turned down Blackberry Lane, the street where Shane Yates lived, a motorcycle went roaring past them, the rider wearing a Hellhound biker cut, with long, curly hair flapping in the wind.

"Do you want to bet that's Yates?" Matt did a U-turn, tires screeching.

"No need to bet." Hannah glanced down at the picture of their suspect. "It's him, all right."

"How did you know he was going to bolt?" Matt asked. Hannah was good and had great instincts, but that bordered on clairvoyance.

"I saw the employee at the front desk that you spoke with make a call while he was watching us leave."

Matt pressed down on the gas pedal, speeding after Yates. "Might've been nice of you to mention it."

"Hey, I told you we needed to hurry over here."

She had, but still… "Full disclosure would've been better."

"Duly noted," she said, with an underlying tone of displeasure.

He could always tell when she disliked something he'd

said to her. This time around working together, calling her *reckless* and uttering *duly noted* were on the list.

Yates glanced back at them and picked up his pace. He took the next corner hard and fast.

Whipping the steering wheel to the right, Matt stayed after him. "I'm sorry I called you reckless. You *can* be—" no doubt about that "—but you weren't last night. To go undercover, alone, to catch the University Killer was gutsy." Still, it irked him, but he couldn't question her bravery or commitment. "And I shouldn't have used such a harsh tone with you when I said 'duly noted' about Farran back at the hospital. I can be overly protective of my people." He took another sharp turn and gunned the gas pedal to keep up with Yates.

Matt flicked a glance at Hannah.

She'd shifted in her seat, facing him, eyes wide, she gaped at him.

He looked back at the road and at Yates. "What? Shocked I'm capable of apologizing?"

"Actually, no. You're the type who would. You care enough about other people. You're empathetic and believe an apology can make a difference. I'm just surprised you noticed those things bothered me."

"I'll make you a deal," he said. "I'll try harder to be less offensive if you try to be less passive aggressive." Yates turned into the parking lot of the Hellhound's clubhouse, and Matt cursed.

Hannah turned to see what had made him swear. "Oh, great. Instead of questioning one Hellhound, now we'll have to deal with all of them."

Yates had parked his bike and ducked inside the building by the time Matt pulled into the lot. He put the SUV in Park, killed the engine and grabbed the handle to open the door.

Hannah placed a hand on his bare forearm, stopping him, her fingers warm against his skin. "I'm sorry, too. For being passive aggressive. When you called me reckless, all I heard was you saying that I was a lousy detective."

"Far from it." He gave her a half grin. "You're the best I've worked with." He thought about Joe, the partner he'd lost, and a pang cut through him. Shoving it down, he got out of the car.

Hannah climbed out and popped some gum into her mouth. She offered Matt a piece, and he declined, not in the mood for bubblegum.

They strode toward the front door, but before they reached it, Todd Burk pushed through, stepping outside, along with two other Hellhounds carrying shotguns.

Todd had been in trouble with law enforcement since they were in high school together, and Matt wasn't too proud of a period when he'd hung out with some of the Iron Warriors. But even as a teenager, no charges had ever stuck to Todd.

The Iron Warriors had given him the fitting nickname Teflon.

"I believe you're lost." Todd gave a Cheshire cat grin, his black hair slicked back, looking every bit the part as leader of an outlaw motorcycle gang. He checked out Hannah, his gaze sliding over her with a sleazy look, and then licked his lips. "It'd be best if you got back in the vehicle and got off our property."

The other two men leered at her as well. Her face and body were lean and honed, but with enough curves to turn heads.

"Not lost." Matt put his hands on his hips. "Here to speak with Shane Yates."

"Don't know anyone by that name," Todd said. "Do

you, boys?" He turned to his buddies, and they shook their heads.

"Knowingly lying to a law enforcement officer during an investigation is a Class 1 misdemeanor, punishable by up to twelve months in jail and a $2,500 fine," Matt said. "You might want to reconsider your answer."

Todd smirked. "I don't even bother to contact my lawyer unless it's a felony charge. Mr. Friedman is way too expensive. And if you haven't learned by now, I don't do jailtime. It's not conducive to my social life."

Matt tipped up the brim of his hat. "I saw Yates run inside through the front door less than sixty seconds ago. I need him to come out and answer a few questions. It's not even about club business. That's all."

With a sneer, Todd shook his head. "You Powells may run this town but not my clubhouse."

Matt took two steps forward. "I'm not a Powell."

"Keep telling yourself that." Todd winked at him. "Now, you look, high and mighty campus police chief, you've got no authority here. Scurry on back to the university before I make you leave. Go on. Get gone."

The other two Hellhounds pumped their shotguns.

Hannah laughed. A great, big, loud chortle rolled out of her as she came up alongside Matt. "That is the most impressive display of testosterone I've seen since the last time I watched *WWE SmackDown*." She pushed back her blazer, unclipped her badge from her belt and held it up to Todd's face. "I'm Detective Delaney, and I *do* have authority here. Send Yates out. Now."

Todd hiked his chin up. "Or what?"

Hannah blew a bubble with her gum, letting it expand in his face until it popped.

She was good. Really good. As they were getting out of

the car, she had expected things to be difficult and planned this little bit of fanfare.

"Or," she said slowly, with that piercing stare of hers that had a way of dissecting someone layer by layer, "I'm going to haul your two sidekicks into jail for obstruction and intimidation of law enforcement officers. And I'm not going to bother with you directly, since you'll simply wiggle out of trouble, as you're prone to do. But I will be back. With lots of other officers. And even if we get to speak to Yates at that point, I'm going to hold a grudge for all the extra effort and paperwork you made me go through. Then it's going to be my mission in life to make things miserable for you and the rest of the Hellhounds." As usual, her voice and mannerisms were clear and direct. Her husky tone was not dulcet, but strong and razor sharp, like barbed wire. "There are going to be raids. Lots of them. When you're riding around, cops are going to pull your guys over if you are this much—" she held her thumb and index finger apart one inch "—over the speed limit. We will invent reasons to search your vehicles, especially those vans that come in and out of this lot. And let's not forget that nettlesome little law that we usually turn a blind eye to—since it *is* the Cowboy State we're living in—that forbids a felon from possessing a firearm. We'll be shining a bright spotlight on you hence forth."

Hannah took Matt's breath away. She was glorious.

One of Todd's buddies, a burly guy with a beard, set his shotgun on the ground and backed up with his palms raised.

Matt loved watching her work—a sight to behold.

"I don't take kindly to threats." Todd stepped up to her, and Matt put his hand on the biker's chest, making it clear he wasn't allowed any closer. "I might have to send a tantamount warning in return."

Hannah lowered Matt's arm and eased forward, going toe to toe with Todd. "It wasn't a threat. It was a promise. And here's a fun fact about me—warnings don't scare me off. They only make me angry."

"You've got spunk, I'll give you that." Todd smiled. "Because I like you and I'm feeling generous, you can have ten minutes if we happen to have anyone inside by the name of... What was it again?"

"Shane. Yates." Hannah gave him a lopsided grin.

"Okay." Todd jerked his head at the man who had dropped the shotgun. The guy with the beard hustled inside the clubhouse.

"And we want to speak to him alone," Hannah said.

"That can be arranged. But only for ten minutes. Not one second longer."

The clubhouse door opened. Shane trudged outside with his head bowed, puffing on a lit cigarette.

Yates fit the basic description of who had attacked Jessica Atkinson in terms of height and build. White. About five-ten. Matt guessed the guy weighed around one-ninety. Pinpointing his age could be difficult. Might be in his early thirties and had simply lived a hard life with too much booze and smoking too many cigarettes. Or he was as old as he looked, late forties. But since the assailant had worn a disguise, his true age was anyone's guess.

"You stay safe out there, Detective Delaney," Todd said with a smirk. "The streets can be rough. Especially for a woman." The Hellhound turned to Matt. "See you around, Powell."

Matt clenched his jaw at the veiled threat to Hannah and being called a Powell. A nasty retort was on the tip of his tongue, but he swallowed the words. The dirtbag wasn't worth it.

"Nice to meet you, Shane." Todd put a hand on the guy's shoulder. "Don't say anything incriminating."

Once Todd and his henchmen were inside, Matt snatched Shane up by the collar with one hand, bringing the biker to the balls of his feet. "Why did your buddy at the transit center need to warn you that we were coming to ask a few questions?"

Shane shrugged. "Just looking out for me, I guess."

"Say we believed that—why the need to run?" Hannah asked.

Another shrug. "I don't know. Because cops don't like bikers."

Matt sniffed around the guy's head. "I smell a lie. Do you smell it?"

"Sure do." With a frown, Hannah waved a hand in front of her nose. "Quite the stench. The next answer you give us better smell a whole lot better, or we're going to continue this conversation down at the LPD. Do you want that?"

Yates shook his head. "No."

Matt let him go. "We've got two questions for you."

"Three," Hannah amended. "For starters."

"Get on with it." Shane took another puff from his cigarette. "What do you want to know?"

"Where were you last night between ten and eleven?" Hannah asked. "And don't tell me it was in this clubhouse, because I won't trust a Hellhound for an alibi."

His shoulders sagged as he squeezed his eyes shut for a second. "I can't tell you where I was."

Better than a blatant lie. But Matt suspected this was where the incriminating part would come in. "Well, you had better, or you're about to become our number one suspect in the university murders."

Yates looked up then, his eyes wide, almost bulging out of their sockets, his face turning pale. "I didn't kill anybody."

Hannah gave a one-shoulder shrug. "Make us believe it."

"What if I was doing something illegal?" He took another drag. "Not anything like murder or rape."

Hannah's gaze slid over to Matt, and he nodded.

"Provided that's true, you've got little to nothing to worry about. Spill it." She glanced at her watch. "*Tick, tock.* We don't have all day."

"I was making my usual *drops*. On campus. Okay?"

Narrowing his eyes, Matt snatched him up again. "Drugs? You're dealing on my campus?"

Yates raised his palms. "They're not kids. They're all adults. Pay in cash. Good customers. They ask me for it. I'm providing a service."

"Let him go, Matt." Hannah put a hand on his arm, coaxing him to comply, and grudgingly, he did.

"Prove it," she said to Yates. "Show us your texts."

If he was dealing and making drops on campus, there would be a digital trail.

Yates took out his phone, unlocked it and showed them his text messages from last night.

It was all there: the requests. Messages that he was on the way. Announcements that he had arrived with their order. The usage of slang and emojis for hydrocodone, oxy, amphetamine, cocaine, Adderall, marijuana, mushrooms, ketamine and GHB.

"You've been selling date-rape drugs on my campus?" Matt asked. "To who?"

"The frat boys, mostly. Who do you think?"

"'Mostly'?" Hannah's brow furrowed. "Has anyone—a guy, older than your usual customers—purchased GHB? Maybe more than once?"

"Uh. Now that you mention it…" Yates nodded. "Weird guy. Real creepy."

That was saying a lot, coming from a drug dealer who associated with the dregs of society.

Hannah pulled out her phone and brought up the picture of the sketch the forensic artist had drawn. "Is this him?"

"Yeah." Yates pointed to the image. "That's 666."

"Why do you call him that?" Matt asked.

"He calls himself that. Wiped out my entire stash of GHB a couple of weeks ago, and before that I hadn't seen him in a while. It's been years."

Shane Yates provided the University Killer with the drugs he used to abduct his victims.

Matt's stomach roiled. He looked at Hannah. "I can't have this guy dealing on my campus."

Alarm swept over the biker's face. "If I don't deal because I talked to you, they'll know I told you, and they'll kill me."

"And we'll promptly arrest them for your murder," Matt said.

"You'd never even find my body. You wouldn't even care if I went missing."

"Don't worry." Hannah patted Yates's cheek. "You'll keep dealing."

"What?" Matt stared at her in disbelief. "No way."

"As my confidential informant," she continued. "You're my new inside man."

Yates shook his head *no*, with a terrified look.

The doors of the clubhouse flew open. Hellhounds began filing out.

"You will," Hannah whispered. "Because if you don't, Chief Granger will shut down your operation and I'll make your buddies believe you're a snitch anyway."

The message was clear. Either way would be a risk to his life.

The Hellhounds mounted their motorcycles—at least ten—cranked their engines and revved them up to a fierce growl. The noise was almost deafening.

Their time was up, and the conversation was over.

Hannah tipped her head in a silent question to Yates, and he gave a subtle single nod.

But neither the biker nor Matt was happy about it.

Chapter Nine

Hannah couldn't believe she was still arguing with Matt. They had been over it, through it and around the issue ad nauseam.

"This is why no one will work with you," he said, his eyes ablaze with anger. "Because you go rogue."

"I prefer to be on my own because of blowback and grief like this. And others don't want me as a partner—which I'm good with, by the way—because I don't play politics. I simply don't care whose feelings get hurt, so long as I get the job done."

But she couldn't run from the fact that she did care about Matt's feelings and his opinion of her. She hated that he was furious, and she hated even more that she was the reason.

"I knew you were trouble," he said, the word stinging her in an unexpected way, like the lash of a whip. "But I didn't think teaming up with you would be trouble for this campus. Do you understand that I'm responsible for the safety and welfare of these students?"

The SAV members had started to arrive for the emergency meeting and were huddled together in the lobby of the Student Union, watching them.

She tipped her chin up at him. "I do understand." Looking around, she took him by the arm over to a corner that afforded them more privacy. "Keep your voice down. This discussion could get a man killed."

"And that man is slowly killing kids at this school." Cheeks red, he huffed out a breath. "You decided to make that guy your CI with flagrant disregard for my job or the position it would put me in."

"That's not true."

He cocked his head to the side. "What are you going to say next? That day is night, the sun is the moon, the sky is purple—"

"And pigs can fly," she said, attempting to lighten the mood, but he only glared at her. "I did take you and your position into consideration. If we stopped that biker from dealing on campus, he would only be replaced by another using different methods. With him as my CI, he's under my thumb. I can make sure that, at the very least, he doesn't sell date-rape drugs on campus anymore. And as my inside person, we might finally be able to take down Burk's entire operation. Put an end to all their drug running and dealing in this town. In the meantime, you can make sure students, like those waiting for us over there—" she pointed to the SAV kids "—are aware that their drinks might be roofied. If I can do something, anything, to limit the sexual assault on campus, I will. I get that you don't agree with my methods, but you did say you'd do this my way. I never guaranteed you'd like it. We're on the same side, fighting for the same thing. I promise you."

Matt drew in a slow, deep breath. "You're right. I don't like it. But they would simply get someone to replace Yates after they killed him for giving up information. He's nothing more than an interchangeable LEGO block to them."

"He's scum for being a dealer, but I protect everyone I work with. Even my informants. Once he sees that and trusts me, I can turn him against the Hellhounds. Against Todd Burk."

"You do realize that you put yourself in Burk's cross-hairs, don't you?"

How sweet that he cared. She was touched. "He's not man enough to come after a cop himself. He'll send some prospect when he thinks I'll least expect it."

Little did the Burks of the world know that she always expected the worst to happen and could handle anything they might dish out.

"It's easy to think that because we're cops, we're un-touchable," he said. "We're not. Dirtbags like Burk can still reach out and hurt us."

No one could ever hurt her more than her father already had. Not with punches and kicks—but he'd bruised and damaged her all the same.

"I know," she said. "I'll be more vigilant. Scout's honor."

He eyed her with mock wariness. "Were you a Girl Scout?"

She smiled. "No, I wasn't. If I had been, I'm certain I would've been kicked out for mouthing off to the troop leader."

"For that or not selling enough cookies. But for sure, they would've booted you out."

They chuckled, and it was nice. Making peace with him. Seeing a sparkle in his eye rather than anger when he looked at her. He had a nice laugh, rich and full and deep. Sexy. But beneath the grin and the light amusement, she saw a sadness in him, lurking behind the perfect facade. Something dark and painful that felt familiar.

And that's what scared her about him. The part of himself he kept hidden.

Looking down at her face, he brushed a lock of her hair behind her ear, stilling her. Gently, he cupped her chin and ran his thumb along her jaw, and she flinched.

Coming to her senses, she pulled away.

He considered her for a long moment. "I get it now," he said, his voice low and solemn.

She wasn't sure if she should ask or even wanted the answer, but the words slipped out anyway. "Get what?"

"That you're more likely to flinch at tenderness than at pain."

It wasn't a question. Simply a bold, insightful statement. One she couldn't deny.

"Chief!"

They turned in the direction of the voice that had called for Matt and spotted Dennis Hill, looking frazzled, holding a stack of flyers and waving his Stetson at them.

"We should get the meeting started," Matt said to her.

"There's no *we* in this. This is your meeting. I'm just a humble spectator."

The corner of his mouth inched up in a grin.

They went over to Hill, who was wearing a black polo shirt with *SWU Police* stitched onto it and khakis—the same as the other members of the support staff she'd seen earlier.

"Doing okay, Dennis?" Matt asked.

Hill was winded. His cheeks were flushed, his sandy-brown hair, which was long enough in the front to brush his forehead, was disheveled and beads of sweat coated his face. "Sergeant Starkey," he said, catching his breath, "had me running around campus, putting these up everywhere." He lifted the remaining flyers in his hands. "By the time I remembered you needed some for the meeting, I was clear on the other side of campus and had to run all the way over."

Matt clapped him on the back. "Good exercise."

Not quite out of shape but with a bit of a belly, Hill wasn't fit, either. Though he had a full head of hair, it was thinning at the top and flecked with silver along the edges.

"That's what I kept telling myself all afternoon." Wiping his brow, Hill smiled. Laugh lines formed around his weary eyes.

"I'll go ahead and get started," Matt said. "While I'm speaking, hand out a few flyers to everyone. Okay?"

"No problem, Chief."

Matt welcomed the SAV attendees, a decent crowd of about forty students. She wished there had been more, but the meeting had been called at the last minute. Although the towns of Laramie and Bison Ridge were small, the university was quite large, drawing almost ten thousand students from Wyoming, across the country and from abroad. Tuition was on the lower end, but the students poured thousands of dollars into local businesses.

Someone cut through the gaggle and put down a one-step stool.

Matt stood on it, and everyone's gaze was on him as he towered over them. He had what Hannah could only describe as *presence*. Any room he walked in, she'd bet everyone would not only notice but also stare a second or two.

A rather distracting trait.

She backed up and leaned against a column as she listened to him speak while Hill handed out flyers for the students to give to others, spreading awareness.

From a distance, Matt didn't lose any of his appeal. Even if it was too much. It certainly had been minutes ago, when he'd touched her. The thought sent another frisson of heat through her, which was silly, considering he'd only caressed her face.

"Don't underestimate the seriousness of this threat," Matt said. "The University Killer has already claimed the lives of ten young women, and we believe he will try to take two more before the month is over. Thus far, he has been targeting petite blondes between the ages of eighteen and twenty-two, but that doesn't mean he won't get desperate and go for a different type. Tell everyone you know. Everyone you see on campus. The more attention and awareness we can bring to this, the better."

Late-day stubble made a shadow of scruff over his cheeks and square jaw. Everything about him was hard yet enticing, from his scruples to his sculpted muscles.

A young redhead raised her hand.

Matt pointed to her. "Go ahead."

She held up the flyer. "If this is a disguise that he's wearing, how are we supposed to know what to look for?"

"A man with his height and build. Possibly asking for assistance or using a different ploy to draw you close to his vehicle, where he can drug you and toss you inside."

Bleach.

Handcuffs.

Leg irons.

A shiver ran down Hannah's spine.

"If you get an inkling that you're being followed, get somewhere safe, with lots of people, immediately. If you find yourself in a situation that feels off in the slightest, get out of there. Above all, use the buddy system. No female student should go anywhere alone, especially at night, until we get this guy. In fact, staying inside your dorms and apartments at night would be best."

"Never going to happen, Chief," said a guy wearing a university hoodie. "This is rush week."

Recruitment week for the fraternities and sororities on campus. Hannah's gut clenched.

Dennis Hill finished passing out the flyers and circled around to her. "This is the chief's first rush week," he said in a whisper, and she recalled Matt had left the LPD in October last year, right after their assignment together, to take the position at the university. "He probably didn't realize because he's been focused on the murder. I'm surprised Sergeant Starkey didn't remind him."

The redhead raised her hand again.

"Feel free to share," Matt said.

"He's right. There's going to be a ton of parties. Everyone goes, whether joining or not. It's the biggest event on campus. Most people I know aren't even planning to attend class on Friday."

Hannah swore under breath. The University Killer went after girls with only a few friends, easier to isolate. It was doubtful he'd go for someone in a sorority. But most kids attended a party or two in college, and apparently, the ones occurring this weekend would have a huge draw for all types. This was going to be a nightmare.

"Then again," Hill said to her, leaning closer and keeping his voice low, "the sergeant is probably still peeved he was passed over for promotion to chief. This is the third time."

She turned to him, and the office manager nodded with a grimace.

"Why are they planning to skip class?" Matt asked.

The same kid in the hoodie laughed. "They'll be hung over, man. The parties kick off tomorrow night."

"Thursday is the new Friday," another student called out.

Nothing good happened after midnight. The kids were dewy-eyed optimists, unaware of the dark side to college parties, which had real consequences. Overdosing. Sexual assaults. Arrests. Blacking out. Driving under the influence. Getting roofied. And too many more dire things she didn't want to consider.

"In the office, we call rush weekend 'the blitz,'" Hill said. "Because it gets crazy with the parties, and the students get quite intoxicated. *Blitzed*. Get it?"

"Yeah." The dread inside Hannah deepened, wrapping around her. "I get it."

"Which reminds me," he said, "I need to get the espresso machine fixed ASAP."

"You might want to call a professional," Hannah suggested.

"I figured out the problem. Needs a new gasket. I'm picking up a replacement on my way home." Hill glanced at the clock on the wall. "I better go before the store closes. Also, I need to get home in time for dinner, or my wife will have a conniption. If she took the time and effort to make the meal, the least I can do is eat it while it's hot. Anyway, you can look forward to an espresso in the morning."

She pulled on a half smile. "Goody."

"There's something else that's come to my attention," Matt said to crowd. "Some of the students, some in fraternities, have been purchasing date-rape drugs. It's easy to slip into your drinks. I'd prefer you to stay home this weekend."

"Not going to happen," someone called out.

Fear of missing out was driving them to attend, when fear of murder should be keeping them in their rooms, playing video games.

Matt sighed. "Only drink what you have poured for yourself. Never leave your cup unattended. If you do, consider it trash and don't drink from it again. For a party, go in groups and leave in groups. There's safety in numbers. Designate someone to stay sober and to account for everyone. This is not the time to trust strangers or to start dating. Spread the word to as many as you can. Let's close the meeting with everyone repeating what I tell you every time."

"Stay alert, stay safe, stay alive," the students said in unison and then began to disperse.

A handful of pretty ladies, including the redhead, stopped Matt, demanding his attention. From the twinkle in their eyes and adoring smiles, they didn't seem to think his brand of appeal was too much. They were fearless in their flirtation.

Did that make her a coward?

Snap out of it, Delaney.

Once he finished speaking with them, Matt made his way over to her.

"You've got quite the fan club," she said, seeing how those girls could be in awe of a handsome campus police chief. A big difference, compared to the college boys.

He shrugged nonchalantly, not showing the slightest interest. "I guess so."

"Most men aren't capable of resisting that. Young, cute, eager to please." For some reason, she was glad he wasn't like most men.

"I sense a compliment buried in there somewhere. But just in case I read that comment wrong, let me set the record straight. If I wanted young, cute and eager to please, I'd get a puppy." His expression turned grim.

Hannah could see the same concern she'd felt earlier, thinking about the upcoming parties, heavy as a boulder in her chest on his face.

"I can't believe I forgot it's rush week," he said.

"You've been dealing with bigger issues, but someone in your office could've reminded you." She wasn't sure if this was the right time to bring up what Dennis had told her.

"It's going to complicate things. I don't know how I'm going to keep these kids safe. Especially this weekend." He ran his hand over the back of his neck. "I need to pop into the office and email Liz's contact, Agent Nancy Tomlinson, what we have so far. Afterward, why don't we grab dinner and hash over the case?"

"I can't. I need to clean out my dorm room and move everything back to my place. For someone who likes to travel light, I can't believe how much stuff I brought." She'd needed more creature comforts than she realized, and then she'd needed things a real college student might've had.

"How about this? You leave your mini SUV—"

"Crossover," she corrected. At least he didn't tease her, calling it a baby SUV like he had last year.

"Leave your *crossover* at the station. We'll take my pickup to the dorm, pack everything in, go to your place, unload it and discuss the case over pizza. Or Chinese. Really anything that delivers."

It had taken her two trips to haul all the stuff. She kept half the cargo space in her trunk filled with emergency supplies. Getting stranded in the middle of nowhere, with limited cell coverage and no essentials—such as bottled water, flares, extra ammo, MREs, blankets, a medical kit, portable charger, two spare tires and her 'go bag' with clothes and toiletries—was never happening to her.

"What about my car?" she asked.

"I'll swing by your place in the morning and pick you up on my way in."

She mulled it over.

"You need to eat," he added.

She did.

"And with rush weekend starting tomorrow…" He shook his head.

The blitz. "Okay," she said. "Since you're providing free labor, I'm buying."

Chapter Ten

Wednesday, September 18
8:45 p.m.

"Maybe you could speak with university administrators," Hannah suggested, seated on the carpet in her living room, resting her back against the sofa. "Explain the gravity of the situation and have the rest of rush week canceled."

If only it was that simple.

Sitting next to her, Matt swallowed the pizza in his mouth and washed it down with a swig of the beer he'd been nursing. His limit was half a beer if he knew he had to drive. "Canceling rush is one thing, which they won't do. Quite another thing to convince students to cancel parties. That's the real draw, not recruitment. The festivities, the music, the alcohol—probably the drugs, too." His gut burned again as he thought about Shane Yates dealing on his campus. But Hannah had made valid points.

The biggest being, this could lead to stopping Todd Burk, the Hellhounds, and their drug trafficking once and for all.

"What if you made it known that you were going to have cops circulating undercover and anyone caught drinking underage would get arrested? I can't think of a better buzz-kill. Parties canceled. One problem solved."

She was thinking like an LPD cop, not one working for a university. "After I accepted this position, my limitations were made painfully crystal clear to me. One of the things I'm here to safeguard is the university's reputation. If the school became known as one that uses a campus resource to give students criminal records, enrollment will plummet. Then there's the practicality of executing such a thing. I'd have to arrest eight out of every ten students. I don't have the manpower, enough space in cells—then there's the logistics, overwhelming the court system." He shook his head. "It isn't feasible."

Hannah grabbed another slice of pepperoni pizza from the open box on her coffee table and picked off the pepperoni before taking a bite. "What about the reputation of having a murderer on campus? They can't be pleased with that. Get them to institute a curfew."

"I don't have enough to justify it yet. The administration is resistant to change."

"What more do you need? Another girl dead?"

He hoped not. "They view this as a failure on my part to do my job. They want this guy caught with minimal disruption to the campus, to the administration and to student life."

She rolled her eyes. "Unbelievable."

"This is my fault, not being prepared for some of the biggest parties of the school year. I should've kept my eye on this while trying to catch the killer. I shouldn't have let it slip through the cracks."

"Hey, there's plenty of blame to go around. I say share it. With Sergeant Starkey." She took a sip of her beer. "He's been with SWUPD for years. He's aware of the parties on rush weekend. Do you know your department even has a name for it? They call it 'the blitz.'"

No. He hadn't heard about "the blitz."

"What was Starkey's alibi?" she asked.

Not this again. "Okay, he didn't bring the parties to my attention, but that doesn't make him a murderer." But it did make him a lousy second-in-command.

"Starkey knows that young women will be extremely vulnerable while there's a killer on the loose. He could've taken steps to mitigate the problem and chose not to. Why?"

"That's a good question."

"Did you know he was passed over for your position?" she asked, eyebrows raised.

"I'm aware."

"Three times."

That, he didn't know. "How are you so well-informed?"

"I'm a good listener." She grinned at him, and he wanted to caress her face, but he also didn't want her pulling away again. "What's his alibi?" she pressed.

"His wife," he said. "She swears they were home together the night Madison Scott was murdered. She has no reason to lie for him. We need to take a closer look at Dr. Foster."

"There's no way he's getting through the winters here in a Z4. Not with all the snow we get." Hannah tipped her beer up to her lips and took a swallow. "I've got an idea, but it's a tedious one."

"Let's hear it."

"We get the DMV records for every dark-colored Tahoe and Yukon that's at least five years old registered in the area. The vehicle had wear and tear on it. Comb through the records and see if he has a second vehicle he neglected to tell us about that matches the description, or if anyone else affiliated with campus does. It's a two-for-one. While checking on him, we might get a lead on a different suspect."

"Do you have any idea how many people drive those

vehicles around here and how long it will take to cross-reference whether they have an affiliation with the campus? 'Tedious' is right. I'll need to dedicate an officer to do it. Then I'll need another to tail Foster to ensure he's sitting at home alone and go through his trash when the opportunity presents itself. I barely have enough to patrol and now cover the campus parties, too." Man power was a serious issue.

She set her beer down and angled toward him, their knees grazing. "I might be able to help with that."

"How so?"

"Chief Nelson told me that whatever I need to get this guy and close the case, I can have. I'll ask for Kent Kramer to keep an eye on Foster."

The guy was a good detective. One of the few to survive the LPD purge of corrupt cops.

"If I can figure out how to be sweet and ask nicely, the chief might even give me an officer for the tedious task of going through DMV records."

Matt put his arm on the sofa behind him, easing closer. As he leaned toward her, his thigh brushed the holstered gun on her hip. "You're sweet. You just don't like to let it show."

"That proves how little you know about me."

He was trying to remedy that. "You have a softer side." He'd seen glimpses of it. "One I find sweet."

She chuckled. "Name one sweet thing I've done."

"You rescued a stray cat we found outside a meth lab and gave it to your elderly neighbor because hers had just died."

"Purely self-serving. Giving her the cat stopped her from knocking on my door whenever she saw my car parked in the driveway and striking up a conversation about drivel because she was lonely."

Hannah lived in a quaint, quiet neighborhood a short

drive from the center of town. In stark contrast to the Shooting Star Ranch and its vast acreage, with no neighbors to be seen for miles, the houses on her street were within spitting distance.

"You keep me fed," he said. "You didn't *have* to get me that protein bar from the café." Some liked saccharine, cloying and in-your-face. He preferred the subtle, nuanced sweetness of Hannah Delaney.

"Once again, I was thinking about myself. I made the mistake of not feeding you later in the day, and you nearly tore my head off in the Student Union over Shane Yates."

He had gotten cranky, as she liked to put it, and had snapped at her. Said things he regretted. "I wanted the pepperoni pizza, so you ordered it, even though you clearly don't eat pepperoni." He gestured to the pieces she had picked off and tossed inside the box.

"You're reaching, Granger. Getting two pizzas would've been wasteful. I'm not sweet. I'm trouble. Remember?"

"You can be both. And some trouble is worth getting into."

She grinned at him. "I think that's the best non-apology I've ever gotten."

He met her honey-brown eyes. Amusement faded from her face, uncertainty taking over. As he took her in, really looked at her, the uncertainty in her expression mixed with awareness, and his throat grew thick.

Like earlier, in the Student Union, they were connected on a different level. Slowly, he grasped her chin and brought her mouth closer. She wasn't beautiful in the classic sense but nonetheless captivating. There was something about her features—the lines and curves of her body, the fierceness of spirit—that lured him in.

He drew closer, stopping a hair's breadth from kissing her. "Sweet trouble," he whispered, aching to taste her.

A soft sigh left her mouth, her bottom lip trembling. "I could use some water." She pulled away, jumped to her feet, and took a step back, both physically and emotionally. "Do you want—"

A crash outside—the sound of glass shattering—had her spinning toward the window and Matt leaping up off the floor.

He looked out the window. Flames danced over the hood of his truck, like someone had thrown a Molotov cocktail. "Stay here," he said, moving toward the front door.

"Like hell I will. This is my house." She cut in front of him, reaching the door first, opened it and stormed outside.

He was right behind her when he heard a rustle coming from the bushes that flanked her doorway.

Whirling at the noise, he faced a man, pouncing from the darkness. The guy charged him, wrapping his arms around Matt's waist, hitting him in the midsection with his shoulder, trying to bulldoze him down. But Matt braced, taking the full force with a groan, grabbed him by his biker cut and tossed him to the lawn. On the top rocker of the leather cut was a Hellhounds patch. The rest was blank. He was a newbie, not a full-fledged member.

From the corner of his eye, he saw a second guy lunge for Hannah. No way for her to stop the tackle; checking a larger, stronger assailant was tough.

At lightning speed, she flowed backward with the blow—using the momentum and his mass to her advantage—and drove her knees up into his abdomen as they hit the ground and flipped him over with her legs.

Before Matt had a chance to be impressed, the other guy charged him again. The same maneuver—head down, shoulder lowered, hitting Matt squarely in the stomach. This time the biker knocked him flat on his back. His attacker landed on top of Matt's chest. The guy got to his knees, quickly sat upright and hit Matt in the face with his fist.

"Nobody messes with the Hellhounds!" he screamed.

Hannah grunted as though she'd been struck hard.

Blocking the incoming blows, he glimpsed Hannah tussling with the other one. Her opponent managed to scramble on top of her and pin her down. She lifted a knee into the man's midsection, which made him gasp and gag. Hannah clubbed her hands together and smashed them against the side of his head, driving him off, and she rolled away.

The wannabe member of the motorcycle gang on top of Matt leaned back, reaching for something in his waistband, but he was having trouble, like it was stuck. Instinctively, Matt realized it was a gun, and if that man succeeded in getting the weapon out, he would die.

Matt reached for the holster on his hip, drew his Glock first and aimed at the biker's center mass. "Hands up!"

A gun fired, the explosive sound of the shot stilling his heart.

Hannah!

"Give me a reason not to put a hole in you," she yelled, and he exhaled in relief. She was okay. "Get face down on the ground with your hands behind your head, and if you so much as twitch, I'll shoot you."

Matt grinned, but a pang in his cheek made him dial it back. "You heard the woman. Down on the ground."

Chapter Eleven

"Thanks for agreeing to do this." Hannah stood in Matt's office in the SWUPD, sneaking glances through the top half of the wall that was glass, across the hall at Matt as he spoke with Sergeant Starkey behind closed doors.

"I didn't agree," Detective Kent Kramer said, sitting in a chair, holding a cappuccino from the espresso machine Dennis had fixed. Instead of wearing his typical frumpy suit, he was dressed down in jeans and a sweatshirt. Good attire for a stakeout or tailing someone. "I'm only following Chief Nelson's orders."

Between doing the paperwork on last night's events in front of her home, getting her request for additional man power approved, persuading her contact at the DMV to assist and reaching out to the homicide division at the Seattle PD—with the time difference, she was waiting on a call back—she'd spent the morning at the Laramie PD with Matt.

"Well, thanks anyway." She handed him a copy of Dr. Bradford Foster's schedule and glanced back over at the other office.

The conversation appeared to be getting heated, at least on Matt's part, as he was doing most of the talking, while Starkey sat looking bored, giving short responses and plenty of shrugs.

"That's quite the shiner you've got there," Kent said, shifting her attention, and he gestured to her bruised face.

The Hellhound had gotten in a few solid punches before she'd been able to draw her gun. Matt had insisted she put ice on the bruise. In fact, he had gotten the chilled compress himself and placed it on her face. And for a few seconds, she'd let him, accepting his tenderness—a vulnerability she didn't let others see. But despite the ice, no amount of makeup was going to hide her black eye. So she hadn't even bothered to try.

"You should see the other guy," she said. "Believe me, it's worse." She gave better than she had gotten, but she could use a couple extra hours of sleep and some more painkillers.

Kent sipped his cappuccino. "I heard those two 'acted'—" he threw up air quotes "—on their own accord and you can't charge Burk."

"You heard correctly." Their lawyer, Mr. Friedman, had miraculously arrived at the station about ten minutes after she and Matt had hauled them in. "Their story is that no one gave them any order to attack me in exchange for becoming full members."

"Don't you mean *kill* you?" Kent asked with a raised eyebrow.

She gave a one-shoulder shrug. "You say potato, I say potahto."

He wrinkled his nose. "I'd like to know how they got your address."

"They conveniently and cleanly had a ready-made answer for that," she said with a wag of her finger. "Found it on the dark web. Sure enough, there's a site out there with my information."

"Anyone else's from the department as a result of the breach, thanks to the dirty former lieutenant?" Kent asked.

"Oddly, no. Only mine. I guess we now know who bought the information." Todd Burk. "Just can't prove it." She couldn't wait to see that man rotting behind bars, right along with most of the town.

Movement across the hall caught her gaze. Matt was up on his feet. Then so was Starkey. Matt had a good four inches on him, but Starkey was solid, with a runner's build.

Kent sighed. "You know, if you throw a frog into boiling water, those suckers just jump right out. But if you place them in a pot full of water that's room temperature and slowly turn up the heat, the frog doesn't notice the temperature change until it's nearly at a boil. And by then…well, it's too late for the poor guy to jump free."

Looking back at the senior detective, Hannah considered what he said. "Am I supposed to be the frog here?" And was the increase in temperature the toll the job took?

He tipped his head to the side with a noncommittal expression.

Hannah appreciated his wisdom but never imagined she would suffer such a fate. "I'll know when the time comes to get out."

"Are you sure about that? By the look of your face, I don't think you do. We all believe we'll know when it's time. Here I am, still in the pot, too, when I probably should've gotten out a couple years back."

The door across the hall swung open, hitting the wall with a clatter. "Why don't you see how well you do without me helping you? Ungrateful SOB." Sergeant Starkey stalked out of the office, no longer wearing his badge or service weapon.

"I think that's my cue to leave." Kent finished his cappuccino and tossed the disposable cup into the waste bin. "It looks like the professor has office hours today." He stood. "Should be simple enough."

Matt came into the office. "Hey, Kent. It's good of you to help out by keeping an eye on Dr. Foster."

"Not really," the older detective said. "I wasn't given much of a choice. The chief told me to come. So here I am. Can I get a map of the campus?"

"Sure." Matt went around his desk and grabbed one. "Here you go. Also," he said, reaching over and getting something else, "this is a permit that'll allow you to park in designated faculty-only spots. By the way, Foster drives a light blue BMW Z4." He gave Kent the license plate number.

Hannah's cell phone rang. She took it out and looked at it. "Seattle area code." She answered, putting it on speaker. "This is Detective Delaney."

"Hi there. I'm Detective Trahern. I got your message about Dr. Bradford Foster. How can I be of assistance?"

"Yes. Thanks for returning my call. I'm here with two colleagues, SWU Campus Police Chief Granger and Detective Kramer. It's my understanding that Dr. Foster helped your department catch the Emerald City Butcher."

"That's not quite how I'd put it," Trahern said. "His assistance did lead to the arrest and conviction of a suspect, Sam Lee. But something felt off to me about the case."

Hannah glanced at Matt and Kent. "Like what?" she asked.

"We never linked Lee's DNA to any of the victims."

Matt scratched at the stubble on his jaw. "Then how did you get the conviction?"

"Trophies taken from the victims were found in Lee's house. He swore he'd never seen them and didn't know how they got there," Trahern said.

"What kinds of trophies?" she asked.

"Their ID cards, jewelry, sometimes underwear."

Matt folded his arms. "Do you think he was framed?"

"No prints were found on any of the trophies in his house. Felt strange to me, but at the time, we just wanted it to be over. I don't know. Sure hope not. If so, that's on me and my partner," Trahern said, his voice rueful. "That brings me to the next thing that hasn't sat well with me. The vast majority of repeat murderers will spill the beans in custody because of their ego—or definitely in prison because if you're a big, bad killer, life behind bars is easier. I've kept tabs on Lee all these years. To this day, he maintains that he's innocent."

"Foster published a book about his work with your division," Matt said, "and takes a great deal of credit."

"I'm well aware. Whenever I see a copy of it, I get sick and want to burn it."

"But the murders did stop once Lee was arrested, didn't they?" she asked.

"Yeah." Trahern blew a heavy breath over the line. "They did. But another way of looking at it is that they also stopped when Foster left Seattle."

Kent shook his head with a grimace. "Were any of the Butcher's victims raped?"

"They were," Trahern said. "But the perp used a condom, and they had all been killed by blunt force trauma to the head. Though there were ligature marks around their wrists, ankles and throats."

"Sometimes these serial killers who have been at it for a while evolve." Kent's mouth twitched. "Get more violent. More sophisticated. Bolder."

"Does this relate to a case you're currently working?" Trahern asked.

"The University Killer has struck on and off for the past ten years," Matt said. "Each time, he abducts three women. All blond and young. Rapes them and strangles them to death."

"The Butcher's victims were young, too—late teens to early twenties—but not all blond. How is Dr. Foster involved?"

Hannah stifled the groan rising in her throat. "He's a person of interest. The murders started a year after he began teaching at the university, at least one victim was a previous student of his, he's come in close proximity to all of them and he doesn't have an alibi. When we questioned him, he tried to flip the script on us and get us to enlist his help working the case."

"That's one slippery, shady dude," Trahern said. "Did you get any DNA from the victims?"

"We did," Matt said. "Our guy didn't use a condom."

Trahern swore. "Then your University Killer isn't the Emerald City Butcher. We found the killer's hair on one of the victims. You would've gotten a match in CODIS."

CODIS, the Combined DNA Index System, was a national database of DNA profiles from convicted offenders, unsolved crime scene evidence and missing persons.

"Even if you clear Foster for your murders," Trahern said, "I would never work with that pompous, self-aggrandizing jerk ever again."

Her thoughts exactly. "Thanks for speaking with us. We won't take up anymore of your time."

"No problem. If you have any other questions, don't hesitate to reach out." Trahern disconnected.

Hannah slipped her phone in her pocket, her mind spinning. Whether or not the professor was their guy remained to be seen. "My gut tells me we're doing the right thing and should still look into him."

"Agreed," Matt said.

"I'll stick to him tighter than a Rocky Mountain wood tick," Kent said, then turned to Matt. "Hey, I never did get a chance to congratulate you on the new job. One day, you were in the office. The next, you were gone. We didn't even get to throw you a going-away party."

Matt shook his head. "Parties are for retirements and promotions."

Kent extended his arms. "This is a promotion. One worth celebrating." He patted Matt on the back, and Hannah rolled her eyes with a sigh.

"Not to everyone." Matt lifted his head, his gaze meeting hers.

Kent waved a dismissive hand in her direction. "Don't let this sourpuss rain on your parade. She doesn't know how to be happy when it comes to herself. Unrealistic to expect her to be happy for others. Delaney will find the one dark cloud in the sky on the sunniest of days."

Wow. Could his opinion of her be any lower? "I'm standing right here. Where I can hear you," Hannah said. "And for the record, I know how to be happy." She just *hadn't* been in a very long time.

"Sure, you do. You wouldn't know happiness if it kissed you on the lips, Delaney. You'd shoo it away, mistaking it for a threat."

She put her fists on her hips. "I believe the phrase is 'If it hit you in the face'."

Kent chuckled. "A Hellhound hit you in the face last night. Did it feel like love? *Poor thing.* Love isn't supposed to hurt."

Yet it did for her. Worse than anything else.

Kent looked back at Matt. "Give me a call one night, and drinks will be on me, Chief Granger. Well, I better get cracking." Kent left as quietly and subtly as he had entered.

"I see your chat with the sergeant didn't go well," Hannah said, desperate to change the topic. Starkey had called him in to show him the surveillance footage of the Mythology class right as Kent had arrived, and things took a turn.

"I'll get to that in a minute." Matt closed the office door and leaned against the desk, crossing his arms as he regarded her steadily. "Kent made a good point. I've worked hard to get to where I am. Why do you begrudge this promotion that I earned?"

Taken aback, she stiffened. "I don't."

"You do. Every chance you get, you undercut it. Imply that I'm some kind of coward for taking it. You literally accused me of *hiding out.*"

Dropping into a seat, Hannah pressed her palm to her forehead. This was a conversation she'd rather not have, but if he insisted, then so be it. "You're the best detective I've ever worked with. Patient and dispassionate when necessary. Shrewd. Gifted at lasering in on perps in a way that I've never seen before. Like you sense the threat. That's exactly what we need out there in the streets. To take down the Burks and the cartels poisoning this town." She looked up at him. The paradox of Matt Granger was eating away at her. "You're a war hero. The most decorated detective in the Laramie PD. What are you doing here if *not* hiding out?"

Chapter Twelve

This time, Matt was speechless. He had no idea she regarded him so highly. *The best detective she'd ever worked with?*

The answer to her question wasn't easy or simple and, now faced with it, wasn't one he was fully prepared to give. He sat in the chair beside her. Tipping his head back, he stretched his long legs.

"I was Special Forces. The job involved a lot of killing and seeing buddies die and others wounded. The job was necessary, and I was very good at it, but it took a toll on me. When I came back home, I joined the LPD. I still wanted to make a difference. Always. And I thought, as a cop here—not like in some major city with a seedy underbelly—that there'd be less bloodshed. That I wouldn't have to lose anybody I cared about to the job anymore."

"And then you lost your partner," she said, her voice soft.

He looked at her and nodded. "We shouldn't have split up. But we did, and a perp got the drop on him. When I got to him, he was still alive. I held his hand and watched him slip away while hearing the ambulance only a few blocks from us. I had to explain this to his wife and his children."

She placed her hand on his arm. "I'm sorry."

"I thought I could push through it—that's what I had been trained to do. But that loss hurt more than the others. Not because he meant more than other brothers-in-arms who died. But I can't shut off my emotions any longer. I lost the ability to go numb. Then we got paired up on the cartel case, and you came so close to dying."

Tightening her grip on him, she rubbed his arm with her thumb, and he appreciated the comfort she offered, knowing it was rare for her.

"I didn't want to go through that again. When this job opened, I jumped at the chance to take it. Because I thought it would be safer. Quieter. No chance of losing anyone else I cared about." Hearing the words out loud, he could no longer deny the truth. "I guess you're right. I *am* hiding out. Or at least, I was trying to. With the University Killer back, I suppose the joke is on me. There's just no escaping the darkness and death." For so long, he'd kept everything bottled up inside, unable to unburden himself. He couldn't talk to his family, and he'd figured he'd never share it with anyone. Until Hannah.

She moved her hand to his cheek. "Not everyone is cut out for this kind of work. But we are. It isn't easy and takes sacrifice. We pay a heavy price for it so that others get to look up at the sky on the sunniest of days without seeing any dark clouds."

That's when it occurred to him: Hannah Delaney had accepted not being happy, probably thinking it was simply a drawback of the job. Plenty of depressed, alcoholic cops to substantiate that belief, but it saddened and angered him at the same time to know that she would deny herself love.

"I was wrong about you taking this job," she continued.

"How so?"

"Yes, you're hiding out, but you didn't have to stay in law enforcement. You could've easily become a full-time rancher," she said, and he had considered it. "Instead, you were drawn to the position because a threat that has eluded everyone else for nearly a decade was coming back, and I think you sensed it. This is where you're supposed to be, right here, right now—to stop the University Killer."

He had been compelled to apply for the job, but he hadn't thought of it that way. Could she be right?

Her gaze slid from his to where her palm caressed his cheek. She dropped her hand, like she just realized that she was touching him, got up and moved away, breaking the connection yet again.

She deserved so much more than she was letting herself have. If only she could see it.

"Was there anything useful on the surveillance video?" she asked.

Shoving down the raw emotions he had allowed to surface, he pulled himself together. "Not really. There was no footage inside the class to see him interacting with Jessica Atkinson—only of him in the hall, hobbling in and out of the room."

She picked up a bottle of water and offered it to him, but when he declined with a shake of the head, she twisted off the cap and guzzled half of it. "What happened with Sergeant Starkey?"

He blew out a long breath. "We got into it after I brought up how he neglected to mention it was rush week, knowing another young woman could easily be taken with all the parties that are going to happen. There was a lot of back-and-forth finger-pointing I'm not proud of, but it became clear that he wants me to fail at this job."

"Did you fire him?"

Matt shook his head. "Nope. He took a leave of absence, effective immediately. Not that I approved it, but he's got a ton of vacation days saved up."

"Better that he's gone."

"This is an all-hands-on-deck kind of situation. The more officers, the better. Now I'm down one."

She finished off the bottle of water. "You don't want to hear this."

"Then don't say it."

"I'm obliged. If it's him, we don't want him to know where officers are going to be placed and what areas will be vulnerable."

"He already has some idea. But I don't think he's the killer. A jerk? Sure. What about his alibi? His wife swore he was home."

Hannah lightly touched her cheekbone and winced. "A person can be home with someone without them actually being home."

"How do you mean?" He got up, grabbed a bottle of painkillers from a desk drawer and tossed them to her.

She caught it. "Boils down to perception. Right? Maybe he was home, at first. They had dinner together. Then he decided to go to the garage and work on a car or into the basement or attic to focus on some hobby, in whatever space he's carved out as his alone. A sacred place. Not to be violated. And while he's in there, no one is to disturb him. Easy enough to turn on a radio or television to mask the fact that he snuck out. Perhaps used a secondary vehicle that he kept parked down the block and killed someone. The entire time, the wife thinks he's home."

He sat back down and stared at her. "That was very, very specific. Alarmingly so."

Averting her gaze, she opened the medicine bottle,

popped a pill in her mouth and swallowed it dry. "Just a supposition that came to me. Anyway, it's possible. Don't you think?"

"Sure. It's possible. Crazier things have happened."

"He's got a hobby, something he's into. Doesn't he?"

Most folks did. "Watching baseball." Nothing suspicious there.

"Games can last late into the night, can't they?"

The latest game he was aware of had gone into eighteen innings and hadn't ended until four a.m. "They can, but she told me that they went to bed together."

"Is that what she said? Or was it more general, more vague? Sort of like, they had dinner, he watched some baseball and they went to bed. That could mean she had dinner with the kids. While he ate in front of the television in the space that's his, where he doesn't like to be disturbed, and she went to bed. When she woke, he was beside her, and she simply assumed that he joined her shortly after she fell asleep."

He honestly couldn't remember the exact wording from any of the statements he'd taken, but he recalled the gist, and Starkey's wife was confident he had been home. "Don't forget, he passed a polygraph test, too."

She shrugged. "Maybe he knows how to beat one. They're not one hundred percent reliable," she said, and he agreed. "Being passed over three times and forced to help the person who has the job you've coveted is a lot."

"'Coveted'? You don't hear that word often outside of church."

"Before you got him riled up, you should've asked him to take a DNA test."

"Not helpful." He shook his head. Unfortunately, Matt would have difficulty getting a warrant for a DNA test at this point since Sergeant Starkey had passed a polygraph *and* had an alibi *and* there was no evidence to justify it. "Maybe we can get Kent to go through his trash, too."

"I'll send a text, asking." She took out her phone and started typing.

"There's something that you should know. I submitted the killer's DNA to a couple of those big, publicly accessible genetic-genealogy-testing services. About a hundred users matched as a distant relative, possibly as close as a third cousin." An ideal match in an ancestry search was a parent, sibling, half sibling or first cousin. It was the DNA equivalent of hitting the mother lode. "Logan Powell, my cousin who works for DCI, connected me with one of their retired investigators to research it, but it could take up to six months to narrow it down to a pool of people who could be the University Killer." The further back the matches went, the more branches on a family tree that would have to be built out. "No one else in the office knows about this. I wanted to keep it quiet. When this guy first started killing women, law enforcement wasn't using the public genetic-testing companies to track down suspects. Now, if our guy got wind that we have tracked down relatives somehow, he might bolt and disappear."

Something close to hurt flashed in her eyes. "But why didn't you tell *me* sooner?"

He didn't really have a good reason. It wasn't anything personal. She could be trusted with the information. "Everything has been happening so fast, one thing after another. Besides, we need to stop this guy before he kills two more women in a matter of days. Does it matter that I'm telling you now?"

Looking away, she shook her head. Her phone chimed, and she looked at the text. "Kent says he'll do it—but wants us to know no one has seen Foster for a few hours. Some students have been waiting to talk to him during office hours, but he's been a no-show. One kid claims he takes off sometimes to go fishing near Gray Reef or the North Platte."

"Have Kent check Foster's house," Matt said.

"Already on it. He's headed that way now." She set her phone down. "As for tonight with the parties, we should do something unexpected."

"What did you have in mind?" he asked, his curiosity piqued.

"Can you call in a favor with your other cousin?"

She would have to be more specific. "Which one?"

"Holden. In the sheriff's department. Nelson can't afford to commit any extra officers to this case. But maybe Holden can spare a couple of deputies tonight. We put them in plainclothes and have them circulate some of the parties."

"That's a good idea." Tonight, they needed as much help as they could get.

Chapter Thirteen

The tempting aroma of a hamburger and fries from the Wheatgrass Café wafted through the car. Parked down the street from the university hospital, where cameras couldn't capture him on surveillance footage, he tugged his gloves back on and pulled the top off the to-go cup of the fountain drink. Cola. He squeezed in a few droplets of tetrahydrozoline hydrochloride, decongestant eye drops easily purchased almost anywhere. In case the cop guarding sweet Jessica didn't drink soda, the water bottle in the take-out bag was his backup method of delivery, which he had already spiked. The top had been opened, but he doubted the officer would even notice.

If he had gotten the dosage right, the cop would only get sick—very sick—rather quickly, sending him to the bathroom to vomit. On the other hand, if he had used too much…

Coma. Seizures. Or even death. None were part of his plan.

Although he'd have to forego his hookup with Jessica, a necessary sacrifice, she was still his prey. Claiming her life was essential. The first punishment for the undercover cop.

Detective Hannah Delaney.

He was going to teach her the hard way—his way—that once he had decided to take something, it was his. The only lives she could save from him were those he chose to forfeit.

Her interference would not be tolerated. And would not go with impunity.

He reached over and opened the glove box. Taking out the small envelope, he smiled.

Since he would not be able to enjoy Jessica in his usual way, she would never be one of his queens. Therefore, he couldn't leave his signature calling card.

Instead, he had something special, unique, just for the detective.

He slipped it into the inside pocket of his thin jacket, which already held the syringe with the lethal dose of GHB.

His cell phone rang. He glanced over at it in the cup-holder and groaned. He'd never answer right before a kill, but he recognized the number and needed to take it. "Hey, kiddo."

"Hey to you, Dad. How are you doing?"

"I'm well." He scanned his surroundings. "You excited for your first rush weekend as a full-fledged fraternity member?"

"Yeah, can't wait," his son said. "So much better than being a newbie, jumping through recruitment hoops. But Mom is driving me crazy. She keeps calling, telling me not to drink and that I'm not at school to party but to learn."

"Give your mom a break. She loves you and just wants you to stay safe, that's all."

"Why can't she be cool about this like you?"

"Moms and dads are different. I trust you to make good choices. You'll find a balance between getting an education and having fun. Only you can figure it out for yourself. We can't do it for you, as much as your old mom might wish we could."

"Talk to her. Tell her that. Get her to back off."

"I can't get her to stop loving you or make her not worry."

"Just wish she'd keep it to herself." Liam groaned. "Are you coming to my frat's parents' weekend?"

"Sure am."

"I'd prefer it if Mom skipped it."

"That's between you and her. I am not getting in the middle."

Another groan. "It's the last weekend of the month."

"I've got it marked on the calendar. I wouldn't miss it for the world."

"Great. I've got to go, Dad. I volunteered to be a sober brother tonight, keeping an eye on things, but first I have to go to a safety meeting called by the council."

"What are you talking about?"

"The campus police chief contacted the council because he's concerned about the safety of the students, specifically the girls," Liam said. "The council asked for volunteers to be sober brothers—watch dogs, really—circulating the party, keeping an eye on things, making sure everyone stays safe."

"Really? Interesting."

"Yeah, and they're beefing up the police presence on fraternity row this weekend."

Good thing he was already ahead of the game. No stopping him. Not tonight. He smiled. "I'm proud of you for stepping up to look out for others. You're a fine young man. Have fun this weekend. Love you, kiddo."

"Me too, Dad."

They ended the call, and he refocused on the task at hand. He needed to get back into character.

Looking in the rearview mirror, he checked his new disguise. He pressed down on the beard, ensuring it wouldn't budge, raked down the hair of the mousy-brown wig over his forehead and tucked down the bill of his cap. Patting his augmented fake belly, he made sure it was secure.

"Here you go," he said, practicing his altered voice. Not quite right. Needed a stronger hint of a Southern accent and to be an octave lower. He cleared his throat. "Here you go, Officer."

Perfect.

He got out of the car and locked the door. Lowering his head in case he passed any cameras on the way, he strolled to the hospital.

In the lobby, he breezed up to the front desk. "Hi there. I've got a delivery order for the SWU police officer on guard duty," he said, holding up the to-go drink and a bag with the words *Wheatgrass Café* written across it.

The attendant smiled. "One moment." She typed on the computer. "Room 411."

"Thanks."

Keeping his head down, he went to the bank of elevators and stepped onto a car behind an elderly gentleman. "Four, please."

The older man nodded and hit the button for him.

When it had reached the fourth floor, the elevator dinged, and the doors opened. He stepped off and got his bearings. Slowly, he walked down the hall, taking note of any rooms that appeared unoccupied. He passed the nurse's station and angled his face away. A few doors down, he spotted the cop, sitting in a chair, preoccupied with something on his phone.

"Evening, Officer. Here you go." He handed the guy the drink and the bag. "Dinner, courtesy of your friends at the SWUPD."

The cop's face lit up like a light bulb, and he smiled. "Thanks. This is better than eating hospital food again."

"Enjoy." He turned and retraced his steps.

Three rooms shy of the elevator, he glanced over his shoulder. The cop had taken the straw from the bag and was inserting it into the fountain drink.

Just as he had hoped.

He ducked into a room that looked empty and slipped inside the bathroom. Keeping his gloves on, he pulled out the clothes he had concealed under his shirt that had been strapped to his body. He slipped scrubs on over everything else he was already wearing, along with a white lab coat. The ballcap, he discarded in the trash. Brand new and purchased while wearing gloves, none of his DNA was on it. He raked down the wig once more.

In a few minutes, the tetrahydrozoline hydrochloride would kick in right around when the hospital would begin their shift change and personnel would be distracted. Timing wasn't just key; it was everything.

Then he'd pay sweet Jessica one final visit.

Chapter Fourteen

Thursday, September 19
7:17 p.m.

With a heavy heart, Hannah stepped off the elevator onto the fourth floor of the hospital with Matt beside her. Officer Carl Farran had been admitted for severe vomiting, blurred vision, difficulty breathing, elevated blood pressure and tremors. Something he'd ingested had most likely been poisoned. He was on the same floor, in room 424.

Hannah and Matt each showed their badge to a hospital security guard who stood outside Jessica Atkinson's room, controlling access as they'd instructed when they got the devastating call about what happened. The guard noted both their names in a log that tracked everyone coming and going. They stepped past him.

The room was so still, quiet as a grave. Hannah went over to the bed and stared down at Jessica's lifeless face. Her brown eyes open, frozen in death.

How?

Hannah gritted her teeth. How had she let this psychopathic killer get to her? Did Jessica know what was happening before it was too late?

There were no signs of a struggle. He must have pretended to be a doctor or a nurse and had injected her arm or the IV bag.

Guilt welled up inside Hannah, making her nauseous. She looked Jessica over, her gaze landing on a small white envelope that had been placed on her stomach.

Hannah glanced around for latex gloves. Matt already had some and handed her a fresh set. She slid on a pair, and he did the same.

As she carefully picked up the envelope, her hand trembled. That monster had rattled her nerves. Deeper than she'd realized.

They examined both sides of the envelope. The back flap hadn't been sealed. With a finger, she lifted it, revealing the edge of a piece of paper tucked inside. Not a playing card, as she had anticipated. Delicately and slowly, she slid the paper free, watching to see if anything fell out along with it, like a hair or anything else. But there was nothing. Only the slip of paper.

On it, three lines had been typed in all caps. It read:

DRESSED TO REVEL, HAZE AND RUN AMOK
CAN'T WAIT FOR SITTING DUCKS LINED UP
NO PALINDROME PALADIN DISRUPTING MY
NEXT HOOKUP

"This psycho had the nerve to write a poem?" Her stomach turned, disgust filling her.

"A tercet," Matt said, and she looked at him in confusion. "A poem with three lines."

"A haiku?"

He nodded, staring at the paper. "A haiku is an example of one, but this isn't that." His lips moved like he was counting. "Each line has seven words but a different number of syllables."

She scrutinized the words. "Revel, *haze*, run amok. He must be referring to the parties for rush. He's planning to take his next victim this weekend, maybe even tonight, and he's taunting us with it."

"Look at the last line. I think it's about you," he said, with concern in his voice. "Your first name is a palindrome, spelled the same backward as forward—and technically, you're a paladin. A guardian. A protector. A warrior."

A wave of anger and frustration rushed over her. "This message *is* for me. He's gloating. Even though I saved her, he still managed to get her in the end. He wants me to feel ashamed that *I*, a paladin, failed to protect her after I promised that I would."

And he had succeeded.

Tears stung her eyes. She swallowed the sudden lump in her throat and placed the poem and envelope in an evidence bag.

"I'm the one who promised." Matt put a steady hand on her shoulder. "This monster got through one of my officers, and that's on me. Not you. Don't you dare think it's your fault."

"That's how it feels." She stared at the poem again. "The way he phrased the last line about me. He's expecting me to fail. He's confident that no matter how hard I try, no matter what I do, somehow, he's going to be two steps ahead of me and grab another woman."

Her nerves tightened at the prospect of that happening. *Not another.* She couldn't bear to lose another one.

"Why didn't he leave a queen of hearts playing card?" Matt said, thinking out loud.

She clenched her jaw, cursing the cruel animal behind

all this. "The poem is so much more effective, don't you think?"

"No, what I mean is, why didn't he leave the card along with the poem?" He stared at the paper, and she could see the wheels spinning inside him. "Almost as though he doesn't consider this to be one of his ritualistic three kills."

Hannah's gut twisted as her heart sank. "Then he only went through the trouble and effort of poisoning a cop and murdering her in her hospital bed, risking exposure and possibly getting caught, just to make me pay for saving her? Because I *disrupted* his *hookup* with her?"

Sweat formed at the base of her spine. Her mind flashed back to the adrenaline-fueled moments when she had stumbled upon him trying to take Jessica. In the hours after the attack, she had replayed the attempted abduction over and over. How she had fought not to let him get the young woman into the car.

All to what end?

She stared at Jessica's cold, pale body. "He's going to rape and murder two more women."

"No. We're not going to let him." He slid his hand from her shoulder to her back. "Do you hear me?"

"What if we are out of our depth, outmatched, outsmarted?" There was no hiding the fear in her voice.

Over the years, she'd learned that a good detective kept their emotions in check no matter how bad, how scary, how deadly things got. She never let anyone see her squirm. Instead, she had always done whatever she needed to do to hold it together and deal with it later, in private.

But standing there with Matt—looking at the woman she'd failed to protect, holding the murderer's provocative message written to mess with her—she couldn't conceal the feelings bubbling over inside.

"This guy isn't as smart as he thinks," Matt said. "We'll get him. One way or another."

She nodded, knowing that it was only a matter of time because the killer had been overconfident and made the mistake of leaving behind his DNA for the past decade. But that sick poem had her second-guessing herself, questioning her next moves.

How was she going to prevent him from taking two more lives?

"While we're here, let's find Nurse Slagle and chat with her about her husband."

"Sounds good." Hannah left the room and went up to the nurse's station. "We're looking for a nurse who works here, Tina Slagle. Can you tell us where to find her?"

"I know Tina," one of the nurses said. "She's off today. My guess is, she's at home, getting in quality time with her kids."

"Thanks," Matt said. As they walked away, he turned to her. "Notice how she said quality time with 'the kids' instead of *the family*?"

"I did. We don't have much time before the meeting with everyone to prepare for the parties tonight. But I think we should make some to swing by the Slagle residence," she said, her thoughts still twisting and churning over that sick tercet.

Dread gnawed deeper at her.

"Hey." Matt caught her by the arm. "Did you hear what I said?"

She shoved the three lines of the poem from her head. "About what?"

"We can have hospital security drop off the surveillance footage at the station. It'll save us enough time to speak to the Slagles." He steered her toward the middle of the corridor to the wall. "I can see that poem is messing with you," he said, and she sighed, unable to deny it. "Last night, you said that I didn't know you well. But there's something about me that you need to understand." Matt drew her gaze and held it. "When I set my sights on accomplishing something, I take dead aim and systematically go over or through everything in my path until I have reached my objective."

She appreciated his efforts to reassure her but was rattled by the idea that Atkinson's death was her fault. "Have you ever been in a battle you didn't think you'd win or survive? And fear wanted to curl you into a ball and try to wish the fight away? You ever felt that?"

"Plenty of times, in the military."

This was a first for her. To not only lose but to also have her nose rubbed in it. "What did you do?"

"Kept my finger on the trigger and my focus downrange, and fought through it. The same way you will now. You're not alone. We'll stop him. You and me, together. I need to hear you say it like you believe it, Delaney. Don't let him into your head. Don't allow him to undermine your self-confidence. Don't let him strip away one of the best parts about you. Your strength. Your will. The way you fight for justice. Because that's what he wants. For you to doubt yourself. You figured out something about him. Enough to run right into him. You did it once. You can do it again. We will stop him."

The other night she had been out on her own. This time, she had a partner. One who'd proven she could rely on him. One she trusted to help her get the job done, even if they had to go into hell and battle the devil himself. "You and me. Together."

As MATT PULLED up to the Slagle residence, which was an easy walk to the university hospital and less than a five-minute drive, Hannah opened one of the buccal DNA test kits that they had in the truck. She tucked the sealed glass vial containing a swab in her jacket pocket.

"Remember," he said, "we'll get more flies with honey."

Hannah grinned. "Well, you said I've got a sweet side. I'll try to tap into that."

Then they went up to the front door. Matt knocked.

A few minutes later, a woman with a messy black bob opened the door. She wiped her hands with a dish towel and slung it on her shoulder. "Hello. Can I help you?"

"Tina Slagle?"

"Yes?"

"I'm Chief Granger." Matt indicated his badge. "This is Detective Delaney. Is your husband home? We'd like to speak with him."

"Actually, he just got back." She opened the door and waved them in. "Come inside."

Hannah offered a small smile. "Back from where?"

"Movie theater. On my days off, I try to give him a few hours of me-time since I'll get mine when everyone else is asleep." She closed the door. "Perry! The police are here." Turning back to them, she said, "May I ask what this is regarding?"

"We're investigating the murders at the school linked to the University Killer," Hannah said as Perry entered the room. "We're examining any possible connections between the victims and trying to eliminate any that we can."

Tina narrowed her eyes. "I don't understand what that has to do with Perry."

"Uh, all the victims had to take my HOPES class," Perry said quickly. "That's all. Nothing to worry about."

"Perry, where were you earlier, between six and seven?" Matt asked.

"Today?" He raised his eyebrows. "I was at the movie theater. Why?"

Hannah flipped to a new page in her notepad. "What did you watch?"

"That silly new action movie," Tina said. "I can't stand the franchise. So Perry always goes without me."

Her husband nodded with a tight grin. "Yeah."

Matt noticed the man wasn't nearly as at ease as he had been at the fitness center, or as talkative. "Were you alone?"

Perry nodded. "Yep."

"Can we see your ticket stub?" Hannah asked.

The guy tipped his head back and to the side. "Uh, you know what? I threw it away with the receipt. After the movie."

A telephone rang in the back of the house. "Elijah! Would you answer that please?"

"Sure, Mom."

Matt smiled. "That's okay. You can pull up your bank account information right now to show us the charge. These days, it pops up like that." He snapped his fingers.

"I can't." Perry stood a little straighter. "I paid in cash."

Tina chuckled. "You never use cash. When did you go to the ATM?"

"Mom, it's the hospital! I think they want you to cover for someone."

Tina sighed. "Excuse me." She left the living room.

Glancing over his shoulder in the direction his wife had gone, Perry stepped closer and then looked at them. "What if I didn't buy the ticket? What if I wasn't alone and I don't want my wife to know?"

"A lot of *if*s." Hannah slid a sideways glance at Matt. "Who were you with?"

"It's a student. I'd rather not say who."

Matt folded his arms. "We need to know so this person can verify your whereabouts."

Perry shook his head. "There has to be another way. Without getting Tina or the student involved in this."

"Unbelievable," Tina said, coming back into the room. "I have to cover for someone. Her boyfriend almost died, and she's an emotional wreck. He's a cop. One of yours, I think." She pointed to Matt. "Apparently, he was poisoned at the hospital, and a woman was murdered." Her eyes got big. "Is that why you're here? Asking where Perry was earlier?"

"We are here to confirm that your husband wasn't involved." Hannah put away her notepad. "Since you can't prove you were at the movies," she said, looking at Perry, "one simple option is to allow us to test your DNA. No one else needs to be involved, and when we speak to the media, we'll be able to say right up front that you aren't a suspect once we have the test results."

Perry glanced at Tina.

His wife shrugged. "Why not? You haven't done anything wrong."

"Sure." Shoulders sagging, he hung his head. "I'll do it."

"Great." Hannah pulled on gloves and opened the vial, and after Perry opened his mouth, she swabbed the inside of his cheek before resealing the swab in the glass tube.

"That's it?" Perry asked.

"That's it," Matt said. "We'll send it off to the lab, and you can get on with your life." For now.

Hannah and Matt left, and they hopped into his truck.

She held up the vial between her fingers. "I've seen perpetrators agree to a DNA test only to run as soon as they're out of our sight. We'll need to get this analyzed as quickly as possible, just in case."

STANDING BY THE large whiteboard at the front of the conference room, Matt was leading the briefing while Hannah sipped on her fifth espresso of the day. He didn't know how she could handle so much caffeine, but she'd shaken off her earlier self-doubt. At least outwardly.

Two of his officers who had worked earlier in the day had agreed to stay for an extra shift, four more cops were scheduled for the evening and Holden had come through with the sheriff's department, providing three deputies in plainclothes. Nine, not including Hannah and himself, was nowhere near enough, but they'd have to make it work. They had no other choice.

"As you know, Officer Carl Farran has been hospitalized, and Jessica Atkinson, the young woman who was attacked, has been murdered. The ME is examining Atkinson's body to determine the cause of death. Doctors have managed to stabilize Carl and are running blood work on him, but they suspect food poisoning. Detective Delaney and I—" he gestured to Hannah "—reviewed the hospital's security footage, and this is what we found."

Matt played the surveillance video on the screen to the right of the whiteboard.

Everyone watched as the University Killer, wearing a new disguise, walked onto the fourth floor of the hospital, handed Officer Farran a drink and bag of food, and then ducked into an empty room. Minutes later, Carl ran to the bathroom in the hall, and the killer then emerged and entered Atkinson's room, wearing scrubs and a white lab coat, and closed the door.

"He timed this to occur around the shift change for hospital staff. The nurses were unaware of what was happening. Less than one minute later, the killer left Atkinson's room. This leads us to believe he injected a drug in her IV."

Hannah stood and held up a photocopy of the poem. "He left this for us instead of his usual calling card." She handed it to the closest officer. "Take a look at it. He's taunting us, telling us that he plans to take his next victim this weekend, perhaps tonight, mostly likely from a party. We need to show him, even though he has been two steps ahead of us, how good we are at playing catch-up."

The law enforcement officers in the room nodded, giving verbal affirmations.

"Ballistics came back on the bullet the killer fired Tuesday night. We got a print but no match to it. This weekend, starting tonight, is another chance to get him. The sororities aren't hosting any parties," Matt said, "but six fraternities are. I've spoken to the Interfraternity Council, four young men who 'govern' the frats. Although they refused to cancel, they want to be a part of the solution. They've agreed to mandate that each fraternity must have five sober members, keeping a close eye on things. Now, I'm a realist. These are kids, not trained cops. I'm not expecting much, but any extra vigilance on their part is appreciated."

The council had also pledged to find out who was using date-rape drugs and put a stop to it, but Matt wasn't holding his breath. Instead, he was going to trust Hannah to do as she had promised.

"Okay, now we're going to go over the game plan and where I want everyone stationed along fraternity row. This is going to be a long night. Parties have been known to last until four in the morning." Groans echoed around the room. "Everyone needs to be fully caffeinated and laser focused."

The conference room door opened, and the junior officer working the front desk poked her head in. "Chief! There's a reporter asking for Detective Delaney's side of the story regarding an incident at her house, and she'd like a statement from you about the murder of Jessica Atkinson."

Before he asked the question, he knew the answer. "Who?"

"Erica Egan."

His pulse spiked. "Tell her 'no comment.'"

The duty officer frowned. "Miss Egan told me to tell you that if you responded that way, I should inform you that you'll want to hear her questions to understand in what light her stories will be framed. She has to submit her DCI story within an hour, and she wants you to have the chance to defend yourselves."

Defend? "Give us a minute," he said to the others in the room.

Matt and Hannah left the conference room.

Her phone chimed. She read the text. "Foster still hasn't gone home yet. Kent has no idea where he could be, but guess what?"

"Tell me."

"Today is trash day for Foster. Kent collected some samples before the waste-management trucks got to it."

"I'll take any good news I can get. I'll ask Logan to get it from Kent. Have the DNA fast-tracked at the DCI."

"But they're notorious for their backlog."

"The governor increased their budget, and DCI recently hired more people so they could handle time-sensitive requests such as this."

"Finally. It's about time. I'll let Kent know." She fired off a quick text to him and shoved her cell phone back in her pocket.

They entered the lobby, where Erica Egan was waiting. The reporter was perfectly groomed, with her hair swept back from her angular face. She wore a low-cut, formfitting sweater the color of ripe mango, tight jeans, high heels and an eager smile.

"How do you know about the incident at Delaney's house?" Matt asked, disgusted.

"Reports of shots fired by the detective during an altercation with two members of the Hellhounds motorcycle club," Egan said, not actually answering the question. "According to the leader of the Hellhounds, Mr. Todd Burk, you instigated the incident after harassing members and trying to coerce them at their clubhouse by issuing unwarranted threats not within your authority. Would you care to give your side of the story?" She shoved a voice recorder forward.

Hannah leaned in, getting her mouth close to the recorder. "No comment. That's Hannah with two h's. Do you need me to spell Delaney for you?" She smiled then, and it wasn't nice.

He hated Egan, but he loved Hannah's style.

The reporter pursed her mouth hard, and lines marred her face. "Don't say I didn't give you an opportunity to set the record straight, Detective."

"'Straight'?" Matt spat the word, full of bitterness. "You slant record, regardless of quotes, and spin stories to influence the public, who you love to claim has a right to know."

"They do." Egan's mouth pressed tight, seemingly offended. "And I'm an objective reporter."

"Cut the bull. All you care about is the number of subscribers."

"My editor cares about subscriber numbers, which have only increased, not only for the paper but online as well since I joined the *Gazette*. Controversy and spice sell, and it keeps getting me bonuses. If you don't like it, take it up with the system." She shoved the recorder in Matt's face.

"Chief Granger, would you care to comment on your failure to safeguard Jessica Atkinson, a student who your department was 'protecting'," she said, using air quotes, "and why the University Killer continues to evade capture?"

Matt swallowed the angry words on his tongue. "The University Killer poisoned a police officer, making him violently ill, and murdered a young woman in cold blood. My department, along with Detective Delaney, will not rest until this serial murderer is stopped."

"Is it true that you're unprepared to keep the student body safe during the blitz of rush because you were unaware this is one of the biggest party weekends of the school year?"

He had hoped that Starkey hadn't gone running to the reporter, but her use of the term *blitz*, was making that seem less likely.

"My officers and I are prepared," he said, "and we will be taking added precautions over the next several days."

"Are you saying that no other students will be abducted and murdered this weekend because of the safeguards you're putting in place?" Egan asked.

"I can't get into the specifics of the measures we're taking, but we'll do our best to keep everyone safe."

"Two women slain thus far with you as chief. Do you think your best is good enough? Are you willing to stake your job on it? If the University Killer strikes again and goes quiet once more, should you resign?"

"We're not gamblers," Hannah said acidly. "We're police officers. Don't forget, the University Killer has eluded other campus police chiefs."

"Yes, that's true." Egan gave a sly grin. "But eventually, they all resigned or were fired from the position. I'm merely asking because readers will want to know if it will be resignation or removal for the current chief."

Matt didn't intend for it to be either.

Hannah's mouth tightened, and her eyes were stone cold. "You're assuming it will be one or the other. We're endeavoring, tirelessly, for a different outcome."

"Chief?" Egan's gaze slid over to him. "Care to add to that?"

"My sole focus at this time is on stopping this murderer and bringing him to justice. That's all I have to say."

Egan switched the voice recorder off. Her smile was feline. "Be sure to read my article. It'll be hot off the presses at three a.m."

Based on previous experience and the way Egan had treated his family in the press, nothing she printed would be good for him, Hannah or the university. "I'll be waiting for it, with bated breath, to use it as kindling for a fire."

Chapter Fifteen

Friday, September 20
3:59 a.m.

The night had gone better than he'd planned. *Flawless.* He had never intended to infiltrate a party and take his prize from there.

Sticking to the list meant choosing a birdie who would be predictably at home. And she had been, too. Her roommate was out, no doubt enjoying the festivities of rush. But he had not expected to find another young girl asleep on the sofa. Taking the blonde without waking the other had been impossible.

Complications were always a possibility. Fortunately, he had been prepared, as always.

He squinted as he scanned the headline of the *Laramie Gazette.* He was bone-tired. But sleep wasn't on his agenda anytime soon. Still too much to do before the sun rose, and then he had a full day ahead of him.

Chuckling, he flipped to the next page of the *Gazette.* They were the fastest with new stories, so he always started with their paper. The timing had given him the chance to get one, along with a coffee, from the last gas station on his way out of town. He needed to go up to the cabin in the woods and drop off his knocked-out cargo for safekeeping.

He glanced over his shoulder and grinned, his mouth watering in anticipation of the hookup to come.

There was time enough for him to take a break. Enjoy his coffee. See what the lovely Erica Egan had to say about him. Then he'd finish making his way to the woods, only to come right back to town. His busy, busy day was just getting started.

He perused the article, wanting to give that sexy crackerjack of a reporter a kiss. Not only had she covered his handiwork at the hospital so eloquently, but she had also bashed Granger and Delaney with electric writing that carried a powerful punch. He pumped his fist in the air.

Laughing, he couldn't wait for Blondie to take a gander. He'd given her a good blow with his poem, and this article would be a hefty bit of salt in the wound.

He sat a little straighter, invigorated, and stopped reading at the bottom of page four. The article delved into a skirmish outside the detective's house, where she had discharged her weapon at 720 Sagebrush Drive.

His jaw went slack. One didn't see that every day.

A police officer's home address printed in the newspaper! A detective's, no less.

Was this luck or serendipity or karma?

No. It was *fate.* He was becoming a true believer in it.

This presented a new opportunity. He cracked his knuckles, thinking. Debating.

Only a fool would pass up a once-in-a-lifetime opportunity like this. He glanced at the red numbers of the clock on the dash. If he was going to do this, in such an unexpected manner, he needed to hurry, even though he much preferred to take things slowly, drawing out his gratification.

But this would be worth it.

Throwing the gear into Drive, he was set on his chosen course. He pulled out of the gas station parking lot and headed back to town.

Chapter Sixteen

Hannah was wiped out and running on fumes. "Thank goodness the night was uneventful," she said as they lumbered back to his office after finishing their after-action debrief with the rest of the officers.

"That we know of." Matt entered his office. "At least on fraternity row."

She followed him inside. "You don't sound pleased by it."

"I am, it's just…when we were out there patrolling, checking on the parties, I kept getting this tingle along my spine. Usually means trouble. Something bad is about to happen."

"No news is good news." They'd even had a couple of security guards posted at the computer lab and rec center as an extra precaution.

"Having the sober brothers circulate the parties turned out to be a good idea by the council. They kept two girls from getting roofied, and the boys who tried drugging those ladies will face charges." He sat at his desk and turned on his computer. "I need to send an update to Agent Tomlinson about Carl Farran and Jessica Atkinson. Once I'm done, want to grab breakfast?"

"I'm starving." She rolled her shoulders and stretched her neck. "Hash browns, scrambled eggs, bacon and toast would hit the spot. Then I need four hours of sleep. Maybe I can get by on two."

"Sounds good. The part about the food," he said, clacking away on the keyboard. "Why not place an order at Delgado's? Then we won't have to wait for it."

She took out her cell phone and called it in. "It'll be ready in ten minutes. The person who took the order recognized my name and kindly put a rush on it since it was law enforcement."

"Ah, the little perks of the badge."

A giant yawn made Hannah's jaw ache. "I'm tired."

"Me too." Matt was still typing at his computer with a slow, methodical rhythm.

He looked bright eyed and professional and not tired in the least.

A newspaper landed on his desk. The morning duty officer stood, glaring.

"What?" Matt asked.

"You're both in the paper."

"We expected to be," Matt said.

"You won't expect what was printed," the officer said in a singsong voice. "Page four, bottom right."

Matt's face tensed.

Hannah snatched up the paper. For a moment, she wondered what awful things the reporter had written about her, especially if the woman had referred to Todd Burk as *mister*. She flipped to page four, looked down at the paragraph on the right and felt the blood drain from her face.

"How bad is it?" Matt asked.

"Worse," she said, her voice barely a whisper. "Way worse than what you're thinking."

Rage spilled over. She fought the senseless urge to tear the paper into shreds and then go find Egan so she could pummel her into oblivion.

"I want to..." She swallowed the rest of the words: *kill that woman.*

First, her address had been posted on the dark web for every creep and criminal to find. Now, this violation. Making it public knowledge for everyone.

Calmly, Matt took the paper from her clenched hands and read it, but his jaw went tight and his eyes blazed fury. "She needs to be fired."

"The editor signed off on it. Allowed it. Printed it. Because the system sucks." She ran her tongue over her teeth. "The paper will hide behind the First Amendment. They can even say it was already posted online."

"That was the dark web." His eyes still flickered with anger. "Doesn't give them the right to pull a stunt like this."

"Egan is a menace."

Matt looked back up at her. "I wanted to talk to you about this anyway. Hannah, you can't stay at your place. I was worried before, with your information on the dark web, but this ups the ante. Every scumbag in town will be prowling around your house, waiting for a chance to do only goodness knows what."

"I'll hang a Welcome sign and set up a lemonade stand. Maybe I can make a few extra dollars."

"I'm serious, Hannah. You have to find a new place to live. Today."

"Not that anyone is asking for my opinion," the duty officer said, "but the chief is right. Ms. Egan painted a bull's-eye on you—or rather, your house. You get what I mean."

Matt nodded. "Yeah, we do."

"Got a genie in a bottle who can snap his fingers and

make that happen? I can't just find a new place out of thin air that fast."

"You can stay with me until you do."

She grinned. "If this is your sly way of getting me into your bed, cowboy, it won't work."

He frowned. "I have a spare room."

"My job here is done," the duty officer said.

"Thanks for the heads-up," Matt said as the guy left.

"I can't stay with you."

"Why not?"

"It crosses a line. Or *blurs* one." The truth was that if she stayed with him, she'd be tempted to break her own rules: Never sleep with someone she worked with. Never spend the night. Never get personal. No strings. Ever.

She'd already gotten way too personal. And she came dangerously close to kissing him when they'd been at her place, discussing a case and eating pizza. And worse, she had wanted to kiss him. Imagined what his lips would feel like, how he'd hold her. She still did.

Dangerous.

"You've got a choice—my place or my family's ranch," Matt gritted out. He shut off his computer. "Let's pick up breakfast and swing by your house so you can pack a bag. End of discussion."

She shoved to her feet, not wanting to discuss it, knowing deep down that he was right.

Her face ached as she climbed into his truck, but she was careful to make sure Matt didn't see her discomfort. They'd been pretty attached at the hip during this investigation. She'd left her car at her house, and they'd been using his truck, which had sustained minor damage from the Molotov cocktail the bikers had used to draw her out.

After they grabbed their order from Delgado's, they

went straight to her house without bothering to eat. Seeing her address publicized had a way of suppressing her appetite. Must've had the same effect on Matt, because he hadn't reached for the to-go bag on the center console between them.

He pulled up in her drive and parked. "You should follow me in your vehicle. Don't leave it here."

"I guess I need to decide where I'm going." She tipped her head back against the seat. "Are you sure your family wouldn't mind putting me up? I don't want be an imposition."

He frowned, casting his gaze down like that wasn't the choice he was hoping for. "Positive. Plenty of rooms. My aunt and uncle would put you in a separate wing from theirs."

"A *wing*? Is *main house* a euphemism for mansion?"

Clenching his jaw, he flattened his lips.

That underbelly was softer than she'd realized. "Why does your dad sleep in the bunkhouse instead of the main house?"

His fingers tightened on the steering wheel. "Because he's the help. He works there."

"But he's also family, right?"

"It's not what he wants," Matt snapped.

"If you don't want me to go to the Shooting Star, then say so."

"I don't want you to feel like I'm twisting your arm to stay with me. I don't want to make you uncomfortable. The Shooting Star is a good option. It's just…"

"Just what?" Hannah studied his face, trying to understand.

"I hate asking my aunt and uncle for anything. I hate being beholden to anyone. For the job is one thing, calling in a favor to save a life. And I'd do it for you." He glanced over at her. "To make sure you're safe."

Something inside her cringed at putting him in such a position.

"Any man who tries to twist my arm will find it gets broken. And you don't make me uncomfortable." Only nervous. And terrified of making a mistake. "No worries about either. You offered your spare room. I'll kindly take it."

He didn't have to care. He didn't have to offer. But he did. What she wouldn't do in the face of that generosity and selfless kindness was insult him by asking him to call in a favor from his family on her behalf.

They climbed out of the truck and went to her front doorstep. She unlocked the door and stepped into the house. It was chilly inside. Had she forgotten to adjust the thermostat?

"Do you mind if I use the bathroom?" he asked, shutting and locking the door behind him.

"No, go right ahead. I'll throw a few things in a bag."

He headed for the half-bath in the hallway. As she made her way toward her bedroom, she noticed a draft in the house. Passing the guest room, she rounded the corner to get to her room and stopped.

Her bedroom door was closed. She'd left it open yesterday. She was certain of it.

She drew the service weapon from the holster on her hip. Raising it, she crept down the hall. At the door, she listened. A slight *whoosh, whoosh* whispered on the other side, in the room. She grabbed the knob, twisted slowly, took a breath and threw the door open.

A crisp breeze slapped her in the face, and the curtains rustled from the window, which had been pried open.

In the center of her bed lay a young blond girl, spread

eagle, her body bare and pale and bruised, her eyes closed. Ligature marks around her neck. A queen of hearts playing card with the eyes scratched out on her stomach. The decorative quilt had been ripped from the bed and the body on top of disheveled sheets, as though he had raped her here. In Hannah's house. In her bed.

Her skin crawled and her stomach clenched. She leaned back on the doorjamb, looking away from the corpse, her heart lodged in her throat.

Near the front of the house, the toilet flushed.

She took one deep breath, fighting against the shock and horror, the sheer revulsion. And then another.

The bathroom door opened in the hall.

"Matt," she called out, her voice steady but not sounding like her own.

"Yeah?" Footsteps hurried in her direction. "What's wrong?"

He came around the corner, and she stepped aside so that he could see.

"No sightings of the SUV?" Hannah asked an officer with the Laramie PD over her cell phone.

"We put out a BOLO as soon as you called in the attack on Atkinson. We also went through all the street cameras in your area once we heard about the next victim, but it's limited," he said, and she gritted her teeth at the truth of that statement. Unlike major cities such as New York, Los Angeles and Seattle, which had thousands of traffic cameras, their town and the surrounding area had the bare minimum. "There's no sign of the vehicle. He must know where the cameras are and is deliberately avoiding them."

"Let me know as soon as—"

"Of course, Detective."

"What about the officer cross-referencing the records from the DMV with those of the university?"

"He's creating a list. He worked sixteen hours yesterday and has been back at it since five this morning."

"Okay. Thanks." Hannah disconnected.

The corpse of Kyra Adams being wheeled out of her house in a body bag. She and Matt had found her student ID card on Hannah's bedside table, along with a second one for a Zoey Williams.

They'd stayed at the crime scene for hours, watching bag after bag of evidence collected and removed.

A crime scene. That was exactly what it was now. Not her home, not anymore. The University Killer had taken that away from her. She didn't want the monster to take anything else.

Hannah paced back and forth while Matt was on the phone with the SWUPD. The waiting clawed at her insides.

"Okay. Thanks." Matt disconnected. "Sergeant Lewis finished speaking with Kyra's roommate, who had been out at one of the frat parties all night. They shared a first-floor apartment on campus. Apparently, Kyra and Zoey had been paired in the Student Support program. It's designed to ease the transition of new undergraduates. The system pairs an older second- or third-year student with a new one. Zoey is only sixteen. She graduated from high school early. According to the roommate, Kyra and Zoey really hit off. Kyra got her into a fantasy tabletop role-playing game and would let her sleep over on the couch if they played late so Zoey didn't have to walk back to her dorm alone at night. Zoey is confirmed missing. Cell phones for both girls were discovered in the apartment, along with their wallets."

That poor girl. To be caught in this sick game of cat and mouse that a psychotic killer was playing.

"Why would he take the other girl?" she asked. "She's not his type." From the picture on the student ID, Zoey had deep-olive skin and dark brown hair.

Matt shook his head. "I don't know. Maybe he was desperate. Didn't want to risk having to go through the trouble of kidnapping another girl later with us searching for him. A two-for-one, and he was willing to make do with a brunette."

Another idea came to Hannah. "Or maybe while he was taking Kyra, Zoey woke up and he had to make a choice— kill her there, subdue her or take her—and he preferred option three." She swore under her breath.

"Since he didn't kill her at the apartment, she's probably still alive. There are usually days between the time when he takes them and takes their lives." Matt put a comforting hand to her back, and she moved away from his touch.

She didn't want to be soothed. Holding tight to fury, frustration and control kept her sharp as a switchblade. And kept her from falling apart. "Tell that to Kyra Adams. She died within hours. Because of me. He saw a chance to do this." She pointed at her house. "To rape and murder another woman I failed to protect in my own home."

This was torture. The way he was terrorizing her by using these women like pawns in a game. One designed to hurt her.

Matt stepped around her, and she looked over his shoulder to see why. He was blocking her from the newspaper photographers taking pictures. "This isn't your fault. It's Egan's. If she had never printed your address in the *Gazette*, Kyra Adams might still be alive. Come on. We need to let Forensics analyze the evidence and the ME examine the body. Standing here, giving the papers more fodder when we're exhausted, isn't going to help anything. Or anyone.

Least of all Zoey Williams. We need to refuel and recharge. Let me get you out of here, okay?"

He was right. Yet again. The last thing she needed was to be provoked and pushed over the edge to the point where she hit a photographer.

"You lead the way," she said. "I'll follow."

Chapter Seventeen

Matt showed Hannah into his house. To call it a *humble abode* would've been accurate. "Look around, and make yourself at home."

She dropped the 'go bag' that she'd taken from her trunk, on the floor near his living room since she couldn't take anything from the crime scene that was at her place and did just that, explored. "Anything off-limits?"

"Nope." He hung up his Stetson.

"Not even the drawers of your nightstand? Trusting me with your wallet is one thing. This could be something else."

A grin pulled at one corner of his mouth. He decided to view her curiosity as interest. "Knock yourself out."

The two-story cabin was simple. The front door opened to a spacious living room, which flowed into a dining room and kitchen. No walls separating the spaces. It was a large, open floorplan, with the exception of an office, powder room and a little den in the back. Upstairs was his bedroom with en suite. Two more bedrooms shared a Jack and Jill bath.

He'd built it not really thinking about the *why* behind

the design. Until Aunt Holly had pointed out it was the perfect layout for a family. Maybe he did have a deep-buried hope—one he'd kept secret even from himself—to one day marry and have kids. Part of him wanted to. He just didn't know how to accept the constant state of vulnerability having a family would put him in.

All he knew was, this place was his, far from everyone else.

But after what had happened to Hannah, he was reexamining the exposure of this location. The one thing about the Shooting Star Ranch was its high degree of safety. The area with the main house, bunkhouse and where his cousins lived was practically a compound, with security cameras and every ranch hand armed.

No one was able to break in and leave a dead body there.

Out here in the boondocks, isolated and far from the Powells, was another story. His aunt and uncle had cautioned him about the choice. Warning him that the Powells had enemies and, by extension, so did he. Cautioning that a law enforcement officer would draw even more threats.

At the time, when he'd picked the parcel of land, he'd dismissed their concerns, only focused on his ego. His determination to stand on his own two feet. His need to carve out something separate from them.

There's safety in numbers.

He'd even advised as much to the SAV group, but here, he was not practicing what he preached.

Hannah waltzed down the steps into the kitchen, where he set out the food. "Nice digs. I wonder what the main house looks like."

"Nothing like this."

"I bet." She took off her blazer and tossed it on top of

one of the chairs that faced the kitchen island. "Got anything to drink?"

"Where are my manners?" He went to the fridge, opened it and pointed to orange juice, a pitcher of iced tea and beer.

"Anything stronger around here? I need a proper drink."

"I need a shower, and you need food before I show you where I keep the whiskey."

"Pretty certain I could find it if I looked hard enough, but I'd like to get cleaned up, too. So once I'm done with my drink, I can just crash for a couple of hours. Can we both shower at the same time?" she asked. "Any issues with water pressure?"

"None, if we're using the same shower," he said, half joking, half testing.

She gave him a soft smile in response, her gaze not leaving his.

"Beyond that?" He shrugged. "I guess we'll find out. I've never had anyone stay over."

"You? Never?"

"Why so skeptical?

"Have you looked in the mirror, Granger?"

He chuckled. "Sure. But what do you see when you look at me?"

Her smile spread wider, and she averted her eyes. "I expect a tumbler of whiskey waiting by the time I'm done upstairs."

He appreciated a woman who knew what she wanted. "Yes, ma'am."

They both hurried through their showers. To his surprise, his was a pleasant one. The water pressure and temperature had been fine.

When she came down to the kitchen, wearing a tiny pair of shorts that exposed a tempting amount of skin, a tank top—sans bra—and with her hair damp and loose, he had built a fire in the living room and poured a drink for her.

"You clean up good," she said, picking up her glass, and he found it hard not to stare.

He gestured to his lounge pants and T-shirt. "If you say so." Then he poured himself a drink.

She eased closer and leaned against the counter. "I do."

"You never did tell me what you see when you look at me."

"A hot guy." Her eyes heated, and his heart turned over. "Who is overtop in the sex-appeal department."

That was unexpected.

He took a step toward her, testing boundaries. She didn't move away, holding her ground, but he could see her pulse flutter at the hollow of her throat. At her side, her free hand flexed and clenched, and he came to an astonishing realization: he made Hannah Delaney nervous.

"You should eat something. Drinking on an empty stomach can impair your judgment faster and could lead to regrettable consequences."

"I'm not hungry," she said dryly. "At least, not for food." Tipping her head up, she regarded him evenly. "Did you really want me to join you in your shower, or were you playing around?"

The moment stretched as he considered a response. Then he decided actions spoke louder than words. With one last single step, he erased the gap separating them. He slipped his hand around her neck, his fingers sliding up into her hair, and kissed her.

She wrapped her arms around his neck as she lifted onto the balls of her feet and kissed him back.

A shudder ran through him, as much from relief as release. It had been a while since he'd held any woman this way, tasted her lips, soaked in the sweet surrender of her response, and he'd wanted to do this with her for days. Careful of her bruised face, he kept it lighter, more tender than he wanted, much shorter than he wished.

Fighting against the coiled want in his gut, he ended the kiss but kept her close in his arms. "I wasn't sure if you wanted this. You've pulled back from me a couple of times."

She pressed her forehead to his chest, her arms curled around his waist. "Sorry."

The word left her so heavily that he drew back to look down into her face. "Why did you?"

Her gaze lifted, those honey-brown eyes glittering with desire as she smiled at him, a heartrending curl of her lips. It was like he'd been sucker punched.

"Because I didn't want to be attracted to you, to *want* you. But I am and I do."

Her response was ego-boosting and concerning all at once. "Why didn't you?" he asked.

"There are so many reasons." She sighed. "I don't know where to begin."

He stroked her back. "Start with the easy ones."

"I have rules. No sleeping with a coworker. No spending the night. No strings attached. But I realized that once this case is over—and it *will* end because we're going to catch him," she said, having regained her indomitable, confident balance, "you won't be a coworker. But you seem like the type of man who cares deeply. That you would for a lover, anyway. It would mean waking up in your bed and lots of strings attached, and things would be messy."

Gently, he cupped her chin between his thumb and index finger. "Messy can be worth it. Sort of like the right kind of trouble." He ran his hand over her hair. "You're a good judge of character, because that's exactly how I'll be with you." No supposition. No doubt. Only affirmation. Flings and casual sex never held much appeal for him. "I'm not looking to take the edge off here. When I'm with a woman, I'm with her. In a relationship. I give as much as I take, but I also expect as much as I give."

He didn't know how to be any other way. Once, things had gotten serious for him. His ex had wanted marriage, and the idea had terrified him. He couldn't commit. At the time, he thought he wasn't the marrying kind because of his mother and the damage of her choices. But holding Hannah, he didn't want to let her go. Funny thing was, he felt like he knew her better, trusted her more than he ever had his ex.

Hannah pulled back a bit. "Here goes the not-so-easy part. I'm not a good judge of character. I'm the absolute worst—in my personal life, anyway. And I've been dreading that you're hiding something. That everything I see isn't what I'll get."

In a weird way, she was proving how well she was able to read him. "I want to work through that. How do we solve it? What do you need from me?"

"Show me yours, and I'll show you mine," she said, and he understood that she meant his soft underbelly. "What's the deal with you and your family? With your father? And the Powells? Why does the subject stress you out and cause you pain?"

This was not a *stand in the kitchen* type of discussion. He grabbed his drink, took her by the hand and led her to the sofa. They sat close, with their thighs touching and her hand on his leg and his palm on her soft, bare knee.

Talking about his family, about the past, wasn't something he did. Easier to keep it locked away. But if he wanted this woman, he'd have to risk the very thing he feared most: being vulnerable.

"My childhood wasn't picture perfect. Things had always been dysfunctional to some extent, with my parents fighting a lot. But my father had been head over heels in love with my mother. No matter the argument or how bad, he made amends, kept the family together, until one day he couldn't. They'd kept the truth from me—that my mom was a gambling addict. She had blown through everything, putting the ranch in so much debt, it was worthless. Then she took off. With another man."

Hannah's eyes softened with pity. "How old were you?"

"Seven. Happened a few days before my eighth birthday." He drew in a deep breath, hating the pain that still surfaced when he thought of it. "Loan sharks showed up. Threatened my father. He offered them the cattle since it was all he had left. They told him that if he didn't get the money to cover my mother's debts, they would kill him and take me as payment. That I'd work for them for the rest of my life. So we left Texas. We ran in the middle of the night. Came here with no place else to go." He took a swallow of his whiskey, embracing the smooth burn down his throat. "My father was a broken man after that, ashamed—a ghost of himself, really." His mother had ripped out his dad's heart and thrown them both away like they were trash. "My aunt Holly took on some of the shame since my mother was not only her sister but also her twin."

"Identical?" she asked.

He gave a curt nod.

"I can't imagine how hard that must've been to be taken in by a woman who looked exactly like the one who abandoned you."

That was it exactly. "Same face. Similar figure. Almost the same voice. But completely different mannerisms and personalities. My mom had been flighty, temperamental, selfish. While Aunt Holly is fierce in her devotion, nurturing, steady, selfless. Her love and affection were a blessing and a curse for that very reason. Made it hard on my dad, too, to be around her. He refused to live in the main house. Grateful that they made him the cattle manager, he chose to live in the bunkhouse, like an employee, and forced me to live with my aunt and uncle in their house, being raised alongside their sons. In a way, he gave me to them and has held himself at a distance ever since."

"How awful." Her voice was thick with sympathy. "Seeing him but not being with him."

"Aunt Holly and Uncle Buck treated me just like I was their son. Anything my cousins got, I got, too. Sometimes they gave me more. Like giving me a parcel of land when only one of their boys will inherit the rest. That's why I'm developing an extra source of revenue—to pay for it in a way." Thinking of how much they'd done for him, given him, made him shake his head with remorse. "I was a fool for not appreciating their love. Instead, I grew up angry and hurt and resentful." If he was honest with himself, he'd admit he was still acting out by choosing to live so far from them.

"I think it's understandable," Hannah said, "considering the circumstances."

"Understandable for a seven-year-old, maybe. Not a teenager. Looking back on it, I regret that I was such a nightmare for them."

"You? I find that hard to believe."

"No, it's true. In high school, I fell in with the wrong crowd because I was stubborn as a mule and determined to distance myself as much as possible from the Powell boys. They were all into sports. I hung out with the Iron Warriors."

Her brow furrowed. "No way."

"Yep. Probably would have eventually joined the motorcycle gang, but when I was seventeen, I got into a bit of trouble. After an argument with my uncle, I ran off. Met up with some of the Warriors. Decided it was a good idea to get drunk. They ended up trying to rob a strip club while I could barely stand on my two feet. I actually passed out in the middle of it. Anyway, the judge gave me a choice because I didn't have a weapon and my blood alcohol content had been off the charts and he considered me to be a Powell, which meant special treatment. Jail or the military."

"That's why Burk kept calling you *a Powell*," she said.

He nodded. "The rest of them got nine years in prison while I got off scot-free."

"You joined the military. Plenty of soldiers have died serving this country," she said, and he had gotten close himself more times than he cared to remember. "You still paid a price."

Matt didn't see it that way. He recognized the leniency shown and the opportunity he'd been given. "I got a GED and enlisted. The army straightened me out fast. By the time boot camp was done, I was a different person. My aunt and uncle were thrilled. Hopeful. Then Special Forces gave me a purpose that I committed to fully." He drained the last of the whiskey from his glass, surprisingly relieved that he'd finally shared the things he'd had bottled up inside all these years. "What about you? Why is your family your soft spot?"

Hannah didn't pull away or try to hide. She simply held his gaze. "In five words? My father is Edward Ressler."

Ressler? Why was the name so familiar? He'd recently heard it. Then it hit him. "The Neighborhood Killer…is your father?"

With grim eyes, she nodded. "I did have a picture-perfect family. At least, I thought I did. Dinners together every night. Church on Sundays. No fighting. My father was my favorite parent. We'd go hiking and fishing, and he'd take me for ice cream on a Tuesday just because. My mother was the bad guy, the one who made me clean my room and do my homework and criticized me for being a tomboy. My father's only rule, the one thing that he demanded, was that we not disturb him when he was in the garage, working on a project."

It was suddenly clear why her example of how Starkey's wife might not have known he wasn't home had been so specific. "Your father would sneak out, take a car that he had parked down the street and…" He let his voice trail off, not needing to say the words.

Sipping her whiskey, she gave a slow nod. "My father was my hero. I looked up to him. Thought he had a noble job, working for a big security company, keeping people safe. He installed security systems in houses. The same homes he later broke into after casing it and programming a backdoor code, murdering his victims."

"Foster said that you were the one to catch him."

"I went into the garage one day while he was out at work. I wanted to tinker around with his things. Be like him. I dropped something. A screwdriver. It rolled, and when I went to pick it up, I accidentally hit a baseboard that was loose. The piece of wood fell. I was going to fix it, but I saw things that he'd hidden behind it. Strange things. Small bundles of hair tied with red string. Driver's licenses that belonged to women."

"Did you understand what it was?"

"Not really. I mean, I was fourteen. At first, with the hair, I thought he had been sleeping with other women and he had keepsakes from them—but when I found the licenses, I knew something was wrong, that it was bad."

"What did you do?"

"I showed my mother. Explained how and where I found those things. For a long time, she sat at the kitchen table, thinking, staring at the stuff I had shown her. Eventually, she looked up the names on the licenses on the computer. She put it together that they were his victims. Then she packed a quick bag for each of us, grabbed food from the pantry and got me out of the house. We went straight to the police station."

He took her hand in his and held it. "That must've been unbearably hard. Grappling with the truth of what your father really was while dealing with the media frenzy at the same time."

She leaned over, resting her head on his chest, and he wrapped an arm around her. "It was devastating. Can't really explain it. Having my whole world collapse. But I guess you understand. Yours fell apart, too."

"It did but not like yours." There was no competition. He'd gotten lucky while she had gotten a raw deal.

"When we first went to the police, I kept telling myself it was a mistake and there had to be some reasonable explanation. Then they arrested him. I thought—as my life imploded and I discovered that my father, who I had idolized, who I thought I knew, became a devil, the true face of evil—that things couldn't get any worse. But they did. The police found a false-bottom space in the house where he stored sick drawings and kept newspaper clippings about the Neighborhood Killer. He confessed to the authorities. Boasted about what he had done. Told them that pressures of being a perfect father drove him to kill again."

"How could he do that to you?" If he had any love in his heart for her at all? "Did you blame yourself?"

"I did. To be honest, even after counseling, there's a little voice inside me that says if I had never been born, those other women never would've been murdered."

"You aren't responsible for his actions." He gentled his tone. "It wasn't fair for him to make you think otherwise." This explained so much about her: How guarded she was. Why she was always looking for a reason not to trust him. The way she so readily took the blame for things that weren't her fault. "You've saved countless people doing your job."

Atoning. For her father's sins and crimes. That's what she was doing, and his heart broke for her.

"The media claimed we must have known. No one believed that we hadn't. It seemed impossible, inconceivable, to them. Once we started receiving death threats, my mom filed for an emergency divorce. The court granted it with no delay. We moved, went by her maiden name after that. She added the h's to my first name to make it harder for anyone to figure out who I really was and dyed my hair blond." She sank against him, and he held her tighter. "Her health started to fail, and right after I graduated from the police academy, she died of a heart attack."

"I'm so sorry." He ached for her loss, for her grief, for the way she had to hide her identity and the worst experience of her life that had shaped her. "I'm glad you're telling me. Finally sharing it."

Knowing the truth of her past only made him that much more protective of her. Not that she couldn't defend herself— Hannah was a force to be reckoned with—but he wanted to shield her from the University Killer's mind games.

The ordeal with her father would only make her more sensitive to his manipulative tactics.

It made Matt long to show that murderer what ranch justice looked like. Where fiends didn't make it to court and were strung up instead.

But then he reminded himself he was a man of the law.

"I haven't been able to let anyone get too close." Her voice was low yet tense. "Not trusting my own judgment. Always waiting for some horrible reveal. But something about you made me wonder if it might be different with you, if I could understand you better. Do you see why I need to be certain that you aren't hiding something terrible about yourself?"

"Absolutely." He put a knuckle under her chin and tipped her face up to his. "You don't know every detail yet, like I leave the toilet seat up and I'm a horrible cook and I've got a thing for beautiful women who rescue kittens," he said, and she cracked a sad smile. "Especially if they're in trouble. But you know everything big and important about me."

She pressed a palm to his cheek. "You swear no nasty surprises?" As she studied his face, a slight tremble went through her. "Because if we try to do this and there are, it'll break me."

His heart started pounding slowly in his chest. He couldn't explain it, how close he felt to her, the undeniable connection after only working on a case together twice. But for the first time in his life, he wanted to give himself completely, fully, to this…budding relationship. "I swear. You're safe with me."

Not taking her eyes from his, she slipped her hand to the back of his neck and lowered his mouth to hers. This time the kiss was savage and greedy. Unrestrained.

He wanted her. In his bed. Under him. Over him. Any way that he could get her. But he didn't want to bulldoze her into anything, either, if she needed to take this slowly.

Mixing the physical with the emotional. A lot was on the line. He didn't want to blow it by rushing. So he pulled his mouth away.

She moaned, curling her fingers in his hair.

"It's been a long day, almost thirty hours with no sleep," he said, making his voice soothing. "If this is all you want right now, me holding you and kissing you, then I get it. I'm not expecting anything more than this."

Smiling and giving him a sexy, predatory look, she climbed onto his lap, straddling his thighs, and there was no hiding how aroused she made him. He groaned, clamping his hands on her hips.

She gripped the bottom of his tee and lifted it over his head. "Well, I'm expecting more, cowboy." Then she pulled off her tank top, tossing it to the floor, baring her full, exceptional breasts and pert nipples to him. "A lot more." She pressed the softness at the apex of her thighs down against the hard ridge in his pants and rocked her hips, making him throb for her. "And I'm willing to sacrifice sleep to have you. Right. Now."

Chapter Eighteen

Friday, September 20
Noon

Pushing up on her elbow in his bed, her leg draped over his, Hannah grinned down at Matt. "You realize we're going to be wrecks for the rest of the day."

"Complete toast." He lay limp and lax, looking sated, with his arm around her waist, keeping her close. Using his fingers, he drew circles on her hip. "But totally worth it. I didn't know how much I needed this."

She slid her palm up his taut washboard stomach to play in the curls on his chest. "How long has it been for you?" she asked softly.

His gaze flicked up to hers. "Four years."

Her eyebrows shot up. "Holy mackerel, that's a long, long time," she said, and he chuckled. She ran her fingers over his muscles, still exploring the lines and contours and every inch of his skin. "I needed it, too."

She had needed him. More than the physical release. A chance to unburden her secrets. To connect, for once. To enjoy this quiet intimacy that she usually denied herself.

But she kept those thoughts to herself. She wasn't ready to share everything quite yet.

He studied her for a long moment. "You deserve this.

To be with someone who wants more than to sleep with you. Who wants to—"

"If you say *take care of* me, I'm going to gag."

His grip on her tightened. "I was going to say *care* for *you*."

And she realized that he did. "While we're working, we have to be just colleagues. Nothing else."

The look he sent her was inscrutable. "Nothing else," he repeated. Then he surprised her by reaching up and kissing her with a fiery hunger that stole her breath.

Fresh waves of desire and need equal in surprise washed over her.

"But later, though," he said, "when we're back in bed, we'll be much more."

She was looking forward to that. Although there was no telling when that would happen.

His cell phone chimed. He reached over. "It's Kent. You haven't responded to his texts."

She swore. "My phone is in the guest room. I should've thought to check it." But she'd been distracted, too busy enjoying Matt Granger and all he had to offer. "What does he say?"

"Foster didn't go back home last night. But he's in class, teaching. Kent has to go home and get some shut-eye. He'll resume watchdog duties this evening."

None of them were machines. She and Matt would probably regret not getting any rest once the adrenaline and endorphins faded.

"How did the handoff go with Logan?" she asked.

"I forgot to mention that my cousin texted while we were waiting for Forensics at your house," he said. "The crime lab at DCI is working on it now."

"Maybe we should hedge our bets. Have someone follow Starkey, too. Just to be sure. The University Killer isn't going to be prowling the parties on frat row tonight or the rest of the weekend."

He nodded. "I think you're right."

"Could you also send one to LPD to help the officer who's going through the DMV records?"

"How about you have your guy come down to the SWUPD?"

She pursed her lips. "Sure."

"We should swing by the ME's office on the way into the station. See if Norris has anything for us."

"Wish we could call the guy."

"Yeah. It'd be nice if he answered instead of letting it go to voicemail. He must get lonely over there. Forcing folks to show up in person." Matt gave her butt a playful smack. "Come on."

MATT AND HANNAH found the medical examiner, suited up, over the body of Kyra Adams in the morgue.

"Hope you don't mind us popping in," Matt said, to be courteous.

Roger Norris always sent an email when he was ready for a visit. But Matt doubted the ME minded.

"Not at all." Norris waved them closer. Behind his forensic goggles, his green eyes were cool and hard. The ME was sharp, efficient and affable.

Matt only wished the guy would pick up the phone more often.

Music was playing; Norris rarely worked without it. Rather than listen to something somber and expected for work that required an admirable constitution, the bluesy, hard rock sound of Aerosmith came from the speakers.

"Here's what I know so far. She was nineteen. Best I can

tell, five-three, five-four. Cause of death is the same as the other University Killer victims, except for Jessica Atkinson—strangulation. She was raped," Norris said.

Hannah shifted uncomfortably beside Matt. He didn't want to imagine what was going through her head. He only hoped she wasn't blaming herself.

"No signs of a struggle," Norris continued, "which would indicate she was heavily drugged and unconscious during the sexual assault and when she was murdered. I've ordered a tox screen. But my guess is, he used his preferred drug of choice, GHB, again. Like he did on Atkinson, with hers being the only lethal dose thus far. We'll know for certain soon enough. There are no secondary wounds or injuries."

Matt's phone rang. He pulled it from his jacket pocket. The weather had dropped about ten degrees, and he'd opted for a leather one. "Granger."

"Hey, Chief, it's Sergeant Lewis."

"Yeah, what's up? I'm at the morgue right now with Detective Delaney."

"Two things. First, the hospital called regarding Carl. He was poisoned with tetrahydrozoline hydrochloride."

"Tetrahydrozo-what?"

"Tetrahydrozoline hydrochloride?" Norris asked, looking up at him, and Matt nodded. "Eye drops. A common decongestant, like Visine or Clear Eyes."

"Did they say anything else?" Matt asked Lewis.

"His drink was spiked with a low dose."

"Could a higher dosage have killed him?"

"I don't know," Lewis said. "I didn't ask."

"Sure could," Norris said. "You know, there have been some recent cases in other parts of the country where a couple of medical professionals used it to off their spouses.

A nurse and an EMT. Both caught. Tetrahydrozoline could also give someone seizures or put them in a coma."

Good thing they were here with Norris.

"What was the second thing?" Matt asked Sergeant Lewis.

"We received a suspicious delivery a few minutes ago. You and Detective Delaney should get back to the station as soon as possible."

Not only did a prickle flare down Matt's spine, but his skin also began to tingle. "We'll be right there."

Hannah was staring at him. "What is it?"

"Nothing good." Of that, he was certain.

SHOVING THROUGH THE front door of the SWUPD, Hannah was right behind Matt.

The duty officer stood. "Sergeant Lewis is waiting for you both in your office with the delivery, and an LPD officer is in the conference room with Farran, going through DMV records and the names of university personnel."

"Carl was released from the hospital?" Matt asked.

"They only kept him overnight. He came in. Says he feels awful about slipping up and wanted to get back to work."

With a nod, Matt said, "Thanks. I need to check on him when I get a moment."

They passed the front desk and headed back. Dennis Hill hopped up from his desk and hurried after them in the hallway.

"Whatever it is, can it wait?" Matt asked.

"I wish it could, but I held off yesterday."

Tension radiated off Matt. "What is it?"

"The bicycle-registration system is down. We can't print any new stickers."

"Students will simply have to wait," Matt snapped.

"You go through the effort of registering bicycles?" Hannah asked. She thought they would have their hands full with other things.

"Yes, we do," Dennis said.

Matt grunted. "Part of the job."

"Many bikes look alike, but identifying one with its serial number is the best way to protect property," Dennis said. "Speaking of which, we can't recover any lost or stolen bikes, either, because we can't access the serial numbers. Sergeant Starkey was working on getting the problem fixed until he left."

A groan rumbled from Matt. "I'll put Lewis on it."

"Thank you." Dennis turned around and went back down the hall.

Entering his office, Hannah spotted the delivery on his desk.

"What's urgent about a box of doughnuts from the Wheatgrass Café?" Matt asked, taking off his hat.

"No one here at the department ordered it," Lewis said, standing in front of the desk. "I questioned the delivery boy. He said that a man came in first thing this morning right as they opened. Placed the order, specified the time of delivery as three thirty-three and told them to include a thank-you card, which he provided."

"Why was the delivery early?" Matt asked.

"There was a lull in customers at the café. The manager told the kid better early than late."

"Did you get a description of the man?" Hannah asked.

"Yeah," Lewis said. "White. Five-ten, five-eleven. Brown hair. Dark brown beard. Baseball cap. Thinks maybe he had a Southern accent. Possibly Texan."

"Sounds like our guy, wearing the same disguise from the hospital," Hannah said.

Lewis nodded. "That's what I thought. When I opened the box, this was inside with the doughnuts." Wearing latex gloves, he handed over a small white envelope with the same dimensions as the one left on Jessica Atkinson's body.

"Oh my God," Hannah said. "It has my name written on it, and this time it's sealed.

Matt moved closer to her. "He wanted to make sure you were the one to open it."

Hannah straightened her spine, bracing for whatever tercet waited inside for her. Turning to the box of gloves, she grabbed some and handed a set to Matt. They both tugged on a pair.

She took the envelope, gingerly opened it and took out the card. Looking over her shoulder, Matt read the type-written note along with her.

TO SAVE ZOEY WILLIAMS AND HAVE HER RETURNED UNHARMED,
 MEET ME AT THE ETERNAL HOPE CEME-TERY BY THE OBELISK TONIGHT.
 7 PM. COME ALONE. OR THERE WILL BE CONSEQUENCES.

MATT CLENCHED A hand at his side. This madman was getting more and more personal with Hannah, dragging her deeper into his twisted games.

"Where is the Eternal Hope Cemetery?" she asked.

"Here," Lewis said. "In the middle of campus."

Confusion darkened her eyes. "Why would they build a graveyard in the center of a university? It's a bit somber for a college setting."

The explanation was a long story, which Matt had learned shortly after taking the job. "The graves were here first. When they decided to build the university, they relocated the bodies. As the school expanded, the graves were moved a second time to what is now the Eternal Hope Cemetery. Deals were made with the town to keep building the university grounds, eventually around it."

"Any significance to the obelisk?" she asked.

Matt shrugged.

"I think the monument is dedicated to young villagers who had died in a skirmish in the late 1800s," Lewis said. "It symbolizes lives cut short."

"Where is it located in the cemetery?" she asked.

"At the center," Lewis said. "Can't miss it."

Matt shook his head. "No, you can't possibly be thinking about doing this."

"He's offered to return the girl unharmed."

"Sergeant Lewis, would you excuse us? And get with Dennis about the bike-registration-system malfunction."

The officer left, shutting the door behind him.

"You can't possibly think he'd simply give her back."

"She's not his type. He wasn't expecting her to be there. But it gives him an opportunity to use that as leverage."

"To what end, huh? Just to meet you?" He shook his head. "I don't think so. There's more to it than that, and you know it."

Looking in her eyes, he could see that she did and simply wasn't concerned with the risk to herself.

"And why at seven when it's still light out?" Sunset wasn't until seven thirty, and the cemetery was a stone's throw from the quad. That early in the evening, the campus would have lots of activity, students walking about, though not through the cemetery. Most steered clear of it because of the ghost stories. "Why not at midnight? I don't like this. Not one little bit."

"Doing this is risky, yes, but if we have a chance to save an innocent girl's life, then we have to take it. *I* have to take it. Or I'd never be able to live with myself if something happens to her when I could've stopped it."

"Regardless of what happens to you?"

"Yes," she said, far too easily, like her life didn't matter.

He understood necessary sacrifice better than most, and this wasn't it.

The familiar prickle that warned him of trouble was now flaring hot. Felt like a live wire being raked down his spine. The last time the feeling had been this strong, his team had walked into an ambush, and he'd lost two buddies.

"This man is baiting you," he said, trying to get reason to sink in for her. "Using your guilt and compassion against you. It's some kind of a trap."

"Of course it is. But there's no other choice if we want to save Zoey."

"He's not going to give up something for nothing in return."

"A face-to-face with me is not nothing," she said, refusing to back down. "You agreed to do this my way."

"But I didn't sign up to let you go kamikaze."

She heaved a breath like he was the one not understanding. "Step away from this case for a second and look at it in a different context. Have you considered that as we get closer to any moment of huge import—huge impact, huge challenge—that human nature tempts us to turn away from it? Sometimes that instinct serves us. But sometimes it's trying to protect what doesn't need protecting and instead is stopping us from taking that very risk we absolutely need to take."

Her point wasn't lost on him. In fact, there had been times in the military before embarking on a dangerous mission where it was easier to focus on why they shouldn't do it rather than why they had to. But she couldn't ignore how her instincts and choices were skewed, because they were going up against a monster that had been like her father. "I agree, but not about this. *You need protecting* when it comes to this guy."

If only she could see how her past made her more vulnerable.

"Why, because we slept together?" She put her fists on her hips. "Great sex isn't going to stop me from doing my job."

The barb stung. It had been more than sex to him. This was the start of something special between them that he didn't want to lose, even if it didn't mean the same to her. "I would never get in the way of you doing your job."

"If this guy wants to meet me in exchange for returning Zoey, then guess what? I. Will. Meet. Him. Getting her back alive is all that matters."

No, Hannah mattered, too. Every life did. But she was sharp and gutsy and made a difference in the world. He wasn't going to let anything happen to her.

"Fine. You'll go," he conceded. "But only over my dead body will you do it alone." His tone brooked no argument.

He would take every precaution conceivable to ensure her safety.

HANNAH WALKED DOWN the road that ran through the middle of the cemetery, the Avenue of Flags. At the center of the graveyard stood the obelisk, pointed toward the sky. It was quiet. No one was around except for the six officers in plainclothes, including Matt and Kent. Everyone had been given a section to cover. Since they had gotten Foster's DNA, Matt wanted to use Kent for this meetup.

The older detective was in his car, parked on the south

side of the cemetery. Another officer was parked on the north end. Matt was concerned the University Killer would somehow lure Hannah to a vehicle, manage to get her in and take off. He was so worried, he'd insisted that she wear a GPS tracker.

No such thing as too careful.

At two inches in length by one inch in width and half an inch in height, the GPS tracker was smaller than a tape measure and fit tucked into her D-cup bra.

"I'm in position," she said into the two-way comms device in her ear concealed by her hair.

"I've got eyes on you," Matt said, his voice steady and husky.

She didn't know his exact location. Only that he had taken a discreet position behind a tree and was watching her through binoculars.

Part of her regretted telling him that it had only been sex for her and nothing more. The idea that their intimacy would change their working relationship had scared her, but she hadn't meant to hurt him. The other part of her understood Matt was a modern-day warrior. A natural protector. His instincts to safeguard someone he cared for would only be amplified, and the only way to prevent it would've been never to sleep with him.

There was no undoing it. Not that she wanted to.

Looking around, she spotted Sergeant Lewis dressed as a groundskeeper, pushing a wheelbarrow. Two more SWUPD officers, making up the rest of the team inside the cemetery, she couldn't see, which was a good thing.

Glancing at her watch, she checked the time. "It's four minutes past seven. Where is he?"

"Patience. He's out there somewhere."

A cell phone rang. But it wasn't hers.

Pivoting on her heel, she followed the sound. There was a burner phone at the base of the obelisk. Warily, she bent down and picked it up. The caller ID stated *Private*. She answered, "Hello?"

"Detective Delaney, how good of you to show up." The voice wasn't as deep as she had expected but was the same as the guy from Tuesday night. Slight Texan accent, barely perceptible.

"Where are you? I thought you wanted to meet."

"I wanted to send you proof of life first. Give me the number to your private cell phone."

"Why do you want my personal number? Send the proof to the burner phone you left."

"Don't give him your number," Matt said softly in her other ear.

"My game," the killer said. "My rules. Unless you don't want proof that Zoey is alive."

"No, I do." Hannah gave him her private number.

Seconds later, her cell phone chimed. A picture of the college student came through. She was seated in the front seat of a vehicle, sunlight filtering in through the window, trees behind her. The girl was dressed in a pin-striped pajama-shorts set that had strawberries on it. Tears filled her eyes. Her wrists and ankles were bound.

"See? She's fine. Not a scratch on her."

"I'd like to see her. In person. Why don't we finish this conversation in person? Isn't that what you want?"

"It is what I want. You were so, *so* close to setting sweet Zoey free," he said, and she cringed on the inside. "But you've hurt my feelings."

"What? How?"

"You're trying to trick me. Like I'm a fool playing your

game and not the other way around. But I expected this from you, Hannah. Because you're deceitful and wicked."

"No, I'm not."

"Yes! You are. And now there must be consequences."

"I'm sorry. Please don't hurt Zoey."

"You're not sorry. Not yet. But you will be once you realize the unnecessary suffering you've caused." He disconnected.

No. What have I done? What will happen to Zoey?

There was no callback number. Still, she clicked on *Private*, trying to dial him back, and received a *not in service* message. Her gut twisted.

A gunshot cracked the air, making her flinch. The impact of the bullet spun Lewis forty-five degrees before he fell. Hannah drew her weapon as she spotted Matt lunge from his position, headed straight for her in a dead sprint.

No, no, no.

Another round whined in, this time hitting Matt, and Hannah's blood went cold.

Chapter Nineteen

The EMT finished bandaging Matt's left arm in the back of the ambulance. "You're very lucky," she said. "The bullet went straight through the muscle. Didn't hit bone. Didn't nick an artery. No fragments left behind."

If only his other officers had been so lucky. Everyone in the cemetery hit had been shot except for Hannah. The murderer hadn't turned his sniper sights on her when he could've easily killed her. Kent and the officer parked on the north side of the graveyard had had their tires and windshields blown out, nothing more.

"Thanks," Matt said to the EMT, then climbed out of the ambulance.

As soon as his feet hit the ground, Hannah's gaze found his. The worry in her eyes was clear and unmistakable.

She was talking to Kent, who was wearing a Kevlar vest. The two headed in Matt's direction, and he met them halfway.

"I'm glad you're all right," Hannah said, her voice soft and somber, and he could tell that she wanted to say more. But she glanced at Kent and took a deep breath. "Your three officers who were taken to the university hospital are going to be okay. Lewis was struck in the shoulder, the other two in the foot and hand."

Matt gritted his teeth, hating that his people had been injured and were in pain but also grateful that they were alive.

"Looking around, the only good sniper vantage from any of the surrounding buildings," she continued, "was the roof of the Animal Science facility and the Sweetwater Recreation Center."

"Laramie PD officers are checking out both now," Kent said, "since most of your guys are out of commission."

Matt shook his head. "This is on me."

"No, it's not," Hannah said. "The note was addressed to me. He gave explicit instructions that I was to come alone and if I didn't, there would be consequences." She was radiating more than anger, something like thundering self-blame. Her expression loosened for only a split second, but he saw what was beneath, how badly she hurt. "Now those men are in the hospital, and Zoey is still out there, trapped with monster."

The sharp-edged rage inside Matt shifted as he realized that he had been so focused on protecting Hannah that he had forgotten to watch out for the rest of his team. "I knew this was some kind of trap or an ambush. I felt it in my bones."

"I wish someone would've given me the heads-up about that," Kent said dryly. "I would've brought my ballistic helmet."

Preparing for something like this used to be Matt's specialty. This failure rested squarely on him. "The cemetery was the perfect location for it. With him having the advantage of the high ground, perched on a rooftop, sighting through his scope, he could not only see all of us but reach out and touch us, too. Pick us off one by one."

"He's got to be a deadeye to shoot like that," Kent said. "Probably a proficient hunter or someone with tactical training."

"Might not be tactical training," Hannah said. "Aren't there a few places within a two to four-hour drive that offer long-range precision-rifle training?"

Kent nodded. "I can think of three. But they're not cheap, if someone wants to learn how to shoot farther than, say, six hundred yards. People spend six to seven grand a day on that kind of training. Won't be paid for in cash, either."

"So they won't be able to give us the runaround about not having records," Hannah said.

Kent tapped his nose with his finger. "They're closed now, but I can make some calls. See if anyone with a university affiliation has been through over the years. I might have to pay them an actual visit to get any real traction."

Matt's phone pinged with an incoming text. "I emailed Agent Nancy Tomlinson about what happened while I was getting my arm bandaged."

"That's the finest example of multitasking that I've ever heard of," Kent said.

"She wants a virtual meeting ASAP. She's emailing a link." The SWUPD had a secure video–telephone software program that was shared throughout the federal government. "She wants to know how quickly we can get started."

Hannah turned to Kent. "Will you take the lead with the LPD cops checking out the rooftops and forensics here?"

"Sure. I can handle it."

Her gaze flicked back to Matt. "Tell Tomlinson ten minutes."

On the walk back to his truck, he sent the text.

Once they reached his vehicle, she held out her hand. "Give me your keys."

"I'm okay to drive."

"Keys," she repeated, her voice firm.

He dropped the keys in her palm.

They climbed into his truck and took off. She switched on the red and blue flashing lights, which gave her the liberty to speed toward the SWUPD while he was seated in the passenger's seat. A first for him. And he didn't like it. But this didn't seem like an issue worth fighting over. Not after the tragic events of the night.

Hannah's mouth was set, her full lips compressed into a thin line of displeasure.

"Something you want to share?" he asked.

"You don't want to know."

Whenever she said that, he'd learned she was right. He probably didn't want to hear what was on her mind. Still… "Just spit it out."

"You were a fool out there," she snapped.

"Come again?" He had been foolish for not doing proper reconnaissance and anticipating a sneak attack, but he didn't expect her to say it, especially not after he'd been shot.

"Running toward me to protect me while a killer is taking potshots with a sniper rifle. *Foolish*. You know better. You're smarter than that. You should've been taking cover. Not further exposing yourself. Did you think my training wouldn't kick in? Did you assume I'd freeze and need you? You didn't charge toward anyone else, hell-bent on saving them. Only me. Yet I didn't get shot."

He exhaled relief over the fact that she was all right. "No, you didn't." He would've preferred to be the one to take the bullet if it meant she didn't have to endure the pain.

"If I had known that you would've acted with such disregard for yourself or that those officers would've gotten shot, I never would have listened to you. I would've gone alone."

"And that would have been a mistake."

"Tell that to the wives and children of your officers who are in the hospital." She whipped the truck into the garage, parked in the spot reserved for the chief and cut the engine. "I told you, when we're outside of the bedroom, we had to be colleagues only. Strictly business. You pretended like you got it. Like you were on board. You lied! I don't want you risking your life for me. I don't need you to do that. I don't need you at all." She reached for the door handle.

"Hold on." He grabbed her wrist, stopping her, and gasped from the lightning bolt of agony that sliced through his bicep.

She winced as though she'd been the one to feel the pain.

"I messed up." On multiple levels. "I did make a promise that I failed to keep. When the gunfire started, the line between colleague and someone I care for evaporated. I've never done this before. It's harder than I expected."

"That's why I don't sleep with people I work with. This was a mistake." In the light from the garage filtering into the truck, her eyes turned impenetrable. "Maybe after this case, we can reassess."

Mistake? Maybe reassess?

He reached over with his good arm, slipping his hand around the back of her neck, brought her mouth to his and kissed her. Deeply. Until the tension drained from her and she softened against him. "I'm not running scared because I was shot. This—whatever it is—brewing between us is not a mistake. It's the first thing in my life that has felt right. Good. I don't need to reassess. Time is precious. People I care about have been ripped from my life without warning. Because they left or they were killed. I could've died today. We both could've but didn't. The fact that we're still breathing, not hospitalized, is a gift. We can't squander that.

I don't want to waste one minute that I could be with you being apart instead."

Tears sprang to her eyes, and a shuddering breath left her lips. "I don't want you to die because of me."

"Well, me neither."

A hiccupping laugh came from her, and tears rolled down her cheeks. She wrapped her arms around his neck and tugged him close. "I just don't want anything to happen to you."

"Ditto. I don't want anything to happen to you, either." He pulled back. "No more talk about mistakes and reassessments. Let's just focus all our energy on catching this guy. Okay?"

Wiping the tears from her face, she nodded. "Yeah."

"You didn't mean it when you said that you don't need me, did you?"

She gave him a sad smile. "I don't want to need you. Because losing you would hurt too much."

He caressed her cheek and kissed her lips.

"Enough," she said, regaining her composure. "Agent Tomlinson is probably waiting by now."

She was right.

They hopped out, rushed into the building and hurried to his office.

He logged into his computer and clicked the link, dialing into the secure video conference. Hannah pulled up a chair and sat beside him.

A silver-haired woman with smooth ebony skin appeared on the screen. "Hello, Chief Granger and Detective Delaney."

"Agent Tomlinson," Matt said, "it's good to put a face with the name. Thank you for this virtual meeting. I'm glad you happened to still be at work."

"I'm always in the office. I keep promising my husband

that I'll slow down so we can enjoy our golden years, but whenever I try, a pressing case finds its way to me. I wish I could've set up this virtual meeting sooner. The more information I receive from you, the clearer the picture. I appreciate the timely updates. Things have escalated far quicker than anything I've experienced in the past."

Hannah leaned forward. "What does that mean?"

"The problem is two-fold. Detective, you interrupted the UNSUB," Agent Tomlinson said, referring to the unidentified suspect, "during his ritualistic process. This has probably never happened to him before, angering and frustrating him. A major blow to his ego. Couple that with the fact that you look like his ideal victim. It's not only alluring to him but also quite vexing in a complex way. Based on everything that you have passed along to me, Chief Granger, I believe the University Killer has developed a fixation on you, Detective. A very dangerous one that he will go to extreme lengths to see satisfied."

Matt clenched his hand. "When you say satisfied, what do you mean?"

"Are you saying that he wants to kill me?" Hannah asked.

"Your death is no longer enough for him," Agent Tomlinson said grimly. "I wasn't certain of that until the unfortunate events of tonight occurred. But now I am. He wants to *eliminate* you in the same manner that he would one of his normal victims."

Disgust roiled Matt's gut. He was never going to let that happen. "We need more information in order to stop him. Why is he only taking his victims from campus? With the attention from law enforcement, wouldn't it be easier for him if he expanded his hunting ground?"

"Easier? Certainly," Agent Tomlinson said. "But he isn't interested in easy. He's interested in besting you. The campus is a place that he loves, enjoys, that makes him feel safe. He's definitely someone affiliated with the university."

"Every time we get a description of him," Hannah said, "he changes his disguise."

"This man is a master at deception. I believe he goes so far as to wear a mask on a daily basis. And I don't mean literally with a physical disguise. I mean not showing his true persona at work or even at home. It's only when he is dominating his victims in his environment, in his lair, that he lets his true self show."

How were they supposed to know what to look for? Matt shook his head in frustration. "You're saying if our killer quacks like a duck and walks like a duck, he might not be a duck."

"As confusing as that may sound," Tomlinson said, "yes."

"Have you found any clues or developed any theories about who he could be?" Hannah asked.

"After what the UNSUB did at the hospital, poisoning Officer—" Tomlinson glanced at her notes "—Farran and then killing Ms. Atkinson without violating her, I had a suspicion. However, it wasn't strong enough to share yet. Although tonight's events have convinced me of my theory."

The back of Matt's neck tingled. An itching prickle that made him rub at it. "Which is what?"

"He is someone who has a love–hate relationship with authority. Specifically with the police. He could have used a lethal dosage of tetrahydrozoline hydrochloride, killing Farran. At the time, I realized it was also entirely possible that he may have guessed how much to use. That's why I kept my theory quiet. But tonight, he had your officers in his crosshairs. He made a choice not to kill any of you. The fact that he only inflicted relatively minor wounds was deliberate."

Matt had wondered about that, if the fact that they had been moving targets had thrown off the killer's aim. "But why, when he could have killed us?"

"I understand it may be hard to reconcile why, in your eyes, a cold-blooded monster who would take the lives of defenseless, innocent young women and not yours. There is a myth that serial killers don't love or care about others. The reality is that some of them often show loving and protective behavior over their own families and those in their inner circle even as they are slaughtering the children of others."

Hannah tensed, clasping her hands in her lap.

Matt knew that must be difficult for her to hear and wished the trauma of her past hadn't resurfaced, but he also knew it was impossible for her not to think of her father.

"That doesn't explain why he didn't kill us," Matt pointed out.

"But it does," Agent Tomlinson said. "You spare that which you care about, even if a part of you also holds it in contempt. His rage and disdain for the police—for the campus police, in particular—is exercised through his killings. Then the question becomes, how do you come to care about something, or someone, you despise? By being in close proximity. By pretending to care on a regular basis until he actually does on some level."

Hannah glanced at Matt before turning back to the screen. "Could it be a police officer? One high up in the ranks, who has been passed over for promotion to chief three times? Even if he passed a polygraph?"

"Most definitely," Agent Tomlinson said with a nod. "Sometimes serial killers are able to pass a polygraph because they don't view the world, the truth, the same way."

Hannah's phone chimed. She read the text. "It's Kent.

Excuse me a minute." She got up and hurried out of the room, disappearing down the hall.

"That brings me to something else," Agent Tomlinson said. "Your guy has an obsessive compulsion around the number three. He's exhibited this in the timing of his kills, the number of his victims. Only choosing months that have exactly thirty days," she said, which was something Matt hadn't realized. "Asking for the doughnuts to be delivered at three thirty-three precisely. But I also strongly believe this will be exhibited in his personal life. Once you pinpoint the right man, it will become obvious on paper. He might have three cars. Three kids. Will use the number three in some deeply personal way that might not seem obvious at first glance."

"Thank you, Agent Tomlinson."

"Wait, wait, there's more. It's about his victims. His choice, blond and petite, is probably related to his mother, who was most likely an authoritarian figure for him. I suspect he tried to reconcile that in his dating life by choosing blondes. Then some woman—a girlfriend, between the ages of eighteen and twenty-one—hurt him, wounded his pride or ego in some way, and she was his first victim. It would explain why he didn't use a condom with his initial kill. He knew her. Violating her was his way of payback, and strangulation is a passionate, personal act. After that, he needed two more victims to fulfill his obsessive compulsion. And for him, there was no reason to use a condom at that point, since he'd already left his DNA on the first body. Look for a personal connection between him and the first victim. That link might not have been evident when he killed her. It's probably the reason he wasn't caught. You might have to go back three months, maybe even three years, from the time of her death to find the connection."

A spark of hope flared in him. "We'll go back over everything related to the first victim."

"Oh, I wish Detective Delaney hadn't left."

"Why?"

"Because I'm concerned for her welfare. Not only does she resemble the type of young woman he goes after and she interfered with his ritual, but she is also an authority figure. This makes her irresistible to him. Then there's the way he violated the sanctity of her home by taking his latest victim there. Raping the girl on the detective's bed," the agent said with a horrified look, "and then murdering her is alarming. Even more so was his elaborate ruse at the cemetery. It was a game. One specifically designed for Detective Delaney to fail."

"I don't understand. You mean he knew that she wouldn't go alone," he said, and as the words left his mouth, a chill snaked down his spine. Of course that monster had known. Otherwise, he wouldn't have been set up on the roof, already in position, waiting. "But why would he want her to fail? He wants to get up close and personal with her, and that was his chance."

"Once again, the answer is two-fold. He expected you and the other officers to be there. By shooting you, he effectively removed her protectors from the gameboard. Isolating her. Then she assumes the failure. The guilt. The responsibility. Not only for the lives of the officers but also for Zoey Williams. He wanted her to fail so that he could give her a chance to atone. To play his game on his terms. I believe Detective Delaney is in grave danger."

Chapter Twenty

"Could it be a police officer?" Hannah asked Agent Tom-linson. "One high up in the ranks, who has been passed over for promotion to chief three times? Even if he passed a polygraph?"

"Most definitely." The senior agent nodded. "Sometimes serial killers are able to pass a polygraph because they don't view the world, the truth, the same way."

Hannah's phone chimed with a text. She glanced down and read it.

Say nothing to Chief Granger or anyone else about this or he dies. I swear it. Leave the SWUPD. Wait for my call. You have thirty seconds.

Her heart squeezed with terror. Pure fear for Matt. "It's Kent. Excuse me a minute." Not daring to look at him and give anything away in her eyes, she got up and hurried out of the room.

Once she had cleared the office, certain Matt couldn't see her, she ran down the hall, past the reception desk, ignoring the duty officer's quizzical stare, and shoved through the doors.

Her phone rang.

"I'm out of the SWUPD," she answered.

"Sixteen-year-old Zoey could still have a bright future. But that depends on what you do next. Do you want to save her?"

"Yes," she said without hesitation.

"Take off your badge and gun. Put both on the ground. If you don't, I'll know."

Glancing around the parking garage, she wondered if he was there, watching her. Hidden in one of the parked vehicles. The two entrances to the garage gave him a second exit so he wouldn't be boxed in. But there were cameras in here.

Instinct had her turning, looking beyond the garage. From where she stood, she could see the street and several parked vehicles. Which meant someone inside of one could also see her.

"Do it," he said, "or the kid will die screaming."

The last time she hadn't followed his rules, four men were shot, including Matt, and Zoey wasn't rescued. The only choice she had was compliance.

She did as he instructed, unhooking her badge and service weapon and then setting them both on the ground.

"Good girl," he said, like she was a dog. "Now, I want you to run to Millstone Cemetery. It's 1.3 miles away. Once you're off campus, take Fifth Street headed west, not Grand Avenue. You have nine minutes, thirty-three seconds to be there, or Zoey dies. Leave your phone. Your time starts now. Run!"

Hannah dropped her phone, pulled Matt's keys from her pocket, letting them fall, and then her legs were moving, pumping as they propelled her through the parking garage. She darted down the road, skirting Fourth Street as she made her way off campus. Taking a right onto Eagle Avenue, she went in the opposite direction of Grand Avenue. She bolted down the sidewalk, her arms pumping, her heart hammering.

Hurry.

Faster.

You have to run faster!

An avid jogger, she was not a sprinter. A ten-minute mile was good for her. Nine was possible. But making it to the cemetery, 1.3 miles away, in less than ten would take everything she had.

The small GPS tracker still tucked in her bra rubbed her skin with each brutal stride she took. In the aftermath of the shooting, she hadn't thought to remove it in the whirlwind of cries, blood, the sirens and then there was Tomlinson's urgent request for a video conference.

Matt would be furious with her for taking off without him. But now she was in the crosshairs alone instead of him being in harm's way. He'd remember the tracker and could find her once she saved Zoey. She didn't care what happened to herself, so long as that young woman survived.

She reached the cross streets of Eagle and Fifth and tore around the corner. Racing down the sidewalk, she dodged pedestrians and darted through traffic, not even slowing for moving cars.

Her lungs were on fire. She could barely breathe. But the one thing that mattered, the only thing, was getting to Millstone in time.

She'd failed Zoey once. Not again.

Hannah's legs were noodles, but a steely determination drove her. The cool night breeze nipped her lungs. Sweat beaded her forehead. Her heart swelled at the sight of Millstone just up ahead.

She dashed across the last street, reaching the sidewalk in front of the cemetery, and suddenly, her legs gave up, bringing her to a teetering halt on the edge of the pavement. She took huge swallows of air, trying desperately to catch her breath and steady her pulse.

A cell phone rang somewhere in the graveyard. She ran inside, down the center lane, searching for the source of the sound, desperate to find it before it stopped.

There!

On top of a headstone was a cell phone. And a capped syringe.

Her mouth went dry, but she grabbed the phone. "Hello?"

"Good girl. You made it with three seconds to spare. I like that. Shows you're committed."

"Where's Zoey?"

"Not so fast. Saving her comes at a price."

She took several more ragged breaths, preparing herself, bracing. "I'll pay it."

"I know," he said, and she could swear she heard him smiling. "A life for a life. Yours for Zoey's. Pick up the syringe, remove the cap, insert the needle in your neck and depress the plunger fully."

Her heart turned to a block of ice.

"I'm watching you very closely. If you try anything funny, if you don't do exactly as I've commanded, Zoey's blood will be on your hands."

"How do I know that you'll let her live? That you'll release her?"

"I wouldn't enjoy a hookup with her. I wouldn't enjoy hurting her, either. She's not really my type. But *you* are."

The words curdled her stomach. "Give me proof that she's alive."

"Zoey, say hello to the pretty detective."

"H-Hello," a shaky, young voice said. "Please help me."

"I will," Hannah said, her heart pounding. "I swear it."

"Describe the detective and what she's wearing," he said.

"L-long blond hair. You're w-wearing a blue jacket and b-blue jeans."

Squeezing her eyes shut for a second, Hannah took a calming breath. She glanced around. A few vehicles were parked on the street adjacent to the cemetery, but no dark SUV that resembled the body type of a Tahoe or Yukon.

"There. You have your proof," he said. "Do as I command."

A cold lance of fear stabbed her, but she shoved it aside. Freeing Zoey was what mattered.

Hannah picked up the syringe with a trembling hand, flicked off the cap and injected herself in the neck.

"Good girl. Now, take off your handcuffs and put them on, wrists behind your back, and wait for me. I'll even let you see Zoey because you've pleased me."

She set the phone on the headstone, took the handcuffs from her belt. Putting her hands behind her back, she slapped them on, loosely enough to be able to slide her wrists free.

With the GPS tracker, Matt would find her in time.

I'll be all right.

No matter what this monster dishes out, you can take it.

I'll be all right. And I've still got the knife hidden in my belt buckle. Given the chance, one split second of opportunity, I'll kill him.

Her vision blurred but then came back into focus. She

swayed on her feet, her head growing heavy, her thoughts clouding. The drug was already taking effect. Quickly.

A white van emerged from the shadow of a building and entered the cemetery, heading slowly toward her.

Squinting against the glare of the headlights, she wobbled, struggling to stay on her feet. Everything turned blurry, her limbs growing numb. A feeling of sludge in her veins slowed down her thoughts, her blood flow, her heartbeat.

The driver's-side door swung open. A man hopped out. It was him. Different wig. No beard. But he had a fuzzy mustache.

She longed to kick his butt, to stomp his face in and make him swallow his own teeth, but as she took a step, everything spun, and she realized her legs had given out and she was falling.

She hit the ground, her head smacking hard against the pavement.

The man opened the passenger door and pulled someone out.

Hannah's eyelids were heavy, so heavy, but she needed to hang on. Long enough to see the girl was okay.

They walked toward her; the girl was crying and barefoot, wearing pin-striped pajamas with strawberries. He shoved her down to the ground on her knees.

Hannah looked up at Zoey's terrified face, and it was the last thing she saw before the darkness closed in.

A DEAL WAS a deal, and he was a man of his word. He picked up the cell phone from the headstone and handed it to Zoey. "Count to one hundred. Then I want you to make a phone call. There is one programmed number. Use it. Ask for Campus Chief of Police Granger. Tell him who you are and where to find you. He'll take care of you. Do you understand?"

"Yes." Sobbing and trembling like a leaf in the wind, the young girl took the phone.

"Fail to do as I command, and I will come back for you. Hurt you. Make you wish you were dead. Understand?"

"Y-y-yes."

"Now, say 'thank you.'" Young people had no manners anymore. He just spared her life.

Tears streamed down her cheeks. "Thank you."

He pulled an extra-long pushpin from his pocket that had a half-inch thick sharp steel needle and pricked the detective in her thigh to be sure she was out cold. Not so much as a twitch from her.

Good.

"Begin counting once I leave the cemetery," he told Zoey, and she nodded, clutching the phone to her chest.

He bent down and scooped up the detective into his arms. As he stood, he braced for the slight pain that flared up. An old leg injury from years ago. One that truly required him to wear a medical boot until it had healed. Sometimes it still bothered him. When it rained. When it snowed. When he had to pick up something heavy from the ground, like a body.

Adjusting her weight in his arms, he carried her to the van. A breeze blew through her hair, kicking up the scent of her shampoo. *Spicy.* Just like their hookup would be.

The detective was a feisty one.

He set her down in the passenger's seat. Then he opened the sliding door on the side. The crisp, powerful scent of bleach curled around his nose, comforting him. He grabbed the detective and tossed her into the van.

Climbing up inside, he looked her over and salivated.

Patience. He removed her boots and patted her down, starting at the ankles, checking for any hidden weapons. This harpy was devious and wicked, and he wouldn't put it past her to have something dangerous concealed.

He ran his palms over her flat stomach and up to her breasts, giving them a nice squeeze. But he found more than supple flesh. Something hard.

What's that?

He pulled out a small, rectangular dark gray transmitter. A GPS tracker. He chained the detective up in the van. Instead of using GHB, he went for something different that wasn't as long lasting because he couldn't wait to party with her. She wouldn't wake up while he was on the road, but he didn't believe in taking unnecessary chances, either. Hence, the shackles.

Smiling, he took the tracker and placed it behind one of the rear wheels. He got into the driver's seat, threw the van in Reverse and rolled over the transmitter as he backed out of the cemetery with his prize secured.

Chapter Twenty-One

"Thank you, Agent Tomlinson," Matt said, grateful for her insight. "But I don't think Detective Delaney can be persuaded to walk away from this case." He was almost certain of it.

"For her own safety, she must. The closer we get to the end of the month, the more aggressive and bolder the killer will become in his effort to achieve his goal. There's no telling how far he'll go. I would also recommend protective custody for her."

The one place he knew, without a doubt, that she'd be safe was the Shooting Star Ranch. "I'll speak with her." Although it would've been better for her to have heard it firsthand from a seasoned FBI agent. Then she might accept the gravity of this threat and not dismiss it as him being overprotective because of his personal feelings for her.

Where was she, anyway? Hopefully, Kent hadn't run into a problem.

"Good luck, Chief Granger. Liz was right to ask me to look at your case. Don't hesitate to reach out if you need anything else."

They disconnected.

Where was Hannah?

He left his office, going down the hallway in the direction she had gone. In the lobby of the station, he looked at the duty officer. "Have you seen Detective Delaney?"

"She ran out of here like the devil was chasing her. Then she stood outside the front door for a minute and bolted."

"What?" He started toward the entrance to see if she had taken his truck. Stepping outside, he saw his vehicle still there.

Then his gaze fell, landing on her gun in its holster, her badge, cell phone and his keys. Disbelief rattled through him as he bent down and picked everything up.

No. Please, no.

"Hannah!" But he knew, deep in his gut, that he was too late.

She was gone.

Fear surged through him, complete and deafening. He reeled against it, his heart stuttering.

He rushed back into the station. "Secure these." He handed the duty officer Hannah's badge and service weapon and slipped her cell phone into his pocket.

Give me the number to your private cell phone.

The University Killer had demanded her personal number so he could continue communicating with her. The text she had received in his office must have been from the killer.

"Call Sergeant Starkey's house," he said to the duty officer. "The landline number, not his cell. See if he's home." This was the quickest, easiest way to see if Sergeant Starkey was a real suspect. The man couldn't be in two places at once. Either Starkey was innocent and at home or he might be the killer and have Hannah chained up somewhere.

With a nod, the duty officer picked up the receiver.

Think.

Think.

The tracker. Maybe she still had it on. Hurrying to his office, he took out his cell phone and dialed Kent.

"Kramer."

"Did you text Hannah about ten, maybe fifteen minutes ago?" he asked, needing to be sure. He sat at the computer and toggled over to the tracking system.

"No, I didn't."

Rage seared through his veins, and he struggled to keep his emotions under control. "That SOB took Hannah. He has her." The program was coming up.

"What? How? She was with you."

The words hit him like a dagger in the chest. "No time to explain. I need you to go to Foster's house. See if he's home. We have to find the killer. Tonight. Understand? We don't sleep. We don't rest. Not for a minute. Until we figure out where he's taken her and get her back."

"Yeah, okay."

Hanging up, he stared at the screen. No green dot. The GPS tracker she'd used earlier wasn't active.

He banged a fist on the desk. Taking a deep breath, he spun out of his chair and went to grab the file on the first victim.

"Chief," the duty officer said, poking his head down the hall, "Starkey's home. Now what?"

"Is he still on the line?"

"Yeah. But not for long. He's about to take his family for ice cream."

Matt raced down the hall and picked up the phone. "Victor, the University Killer shot three campus officers and me tonight," he said, bypassing any pleasantries and using Starkey's first name, to hit home that this attack on them was personal. "The others are in the hospital. I believe he's taken Detective Delaney. Your leave of absence is over, effective immediately. I need you here now. Uniform doesn't matter."

"On my way, Chief. I'll be there in ten."

Matt slammed the phone down on the receiver. As he was leaving to go grab the file, the phone rang.

The duty officer answered at the front and then called back to him. "Chief, it's for you. Sounds urgent."

Maybe it was him. The killer. Calling to gloat. To ask for something in exchange for Hannah. He put the phone to his ear. "This is Chief Granger."

"M-m-my name is Zoey Williams. He told me to call you. Only you. That you would make sure I was safe."

Grim calmness stole over him. "Detective Hannah Delaney. Did you see her? Do you know where she is?"

"He took her. The blond detective. He said 'a life for a life.'"

His stomach upheaved. Matt couldn't regret that an innocent teen had been released. But he also couldn't— wouldn't—accept this sacrifice that Hannah had made. He would do whatever necessary to get her back. "Where are you?"

"I don't know. A cemetery. Stone-something. I see a street sign for Grand Avenue."

"The Millstone Cemetery?"

"Yeah, I think that's it."

"I'm sending a cop to come and get you." While Matt would dig into the file on the first victim. "He'll be there in less than five minutes. In the meantime, I'm going to put the duty officer back on the phone. He's going to talk to you until you're in a patrol car. Okay?"

She sobbed over the line. "Thank you. Please hurry."

HE PARKED THE van at the cabin in the woods, which was only a thirty-minute drive from town, and slung Delaney over his shoulder. Walking past the front steps of the cabin, he went around to the side of the house. He squatted, grimacing against the ache in his leg. After removing the padlock, he opened the door to the soundproof, self-sealing concrete storm shelter. What he liked to call "the party room."

Balancing her weight on his shoulder, he eased down the steps.

Sometimes he brought his son out to the woods to hunt deer and elk, but no one was allowed down here. This was his special place, and only he had the key for the padlock.

He flopped Delaney on top of the fresh sheets and blanket covering the cot that was bolted to the floor. A proper hookup always had to start with clean white bedding. That way he could enjoy seeing it get dirty.

Snickering, he uncuffed her. But she wouldn't be unrestrained for long. He unbuckled her belt, unzipped her jeans, peeled them off, removed her jacket and T-shirt, undressing her down to her underwear. He ran his hands over her body. She would do nicely. When she woke up, she would realize her place in this new world—his world, where he would be her god.

"FOSTER IS HOME," Kent said over the phone. "He's watching a cooking show. Drinking pinot noir. I'm headed back to campus. Almost there."

Matt slapped the file in front of him closed. "Thanks. I rechecked the case file on the first victim, Paige Johnson. She was nineteen when she was killed. I spoke with her father. He said Paige didn't have any boyfriends."

"Do you believe him?"

"Paige liked girls, according to her father. So yes. He

also said she got along with everybody. Never had any nega-
tive run-ins with anyone." Matt sighed. "Agent Tomlinson
was confident there is a personal connection between the
first victim and the killer."

What was he missing?

He was peeling away layers of the puzzle, but he didn't
have the core. Not yet. It was only a matter of time. He just
didn't know how much Hannah had.

Starkey flung open Matt's office door and rushed in with
Carl and the LPD officer.

"Did you find something?" Matt asked.

"Possibly," Starkey said, his face grave. "There are quite
a few people working at the university who drive a dark
Tahoe or Yukon. But Carl noticed something odd."

Matt put his cell on speaker so Kent could stay in the
loop. "What is it?"

Starkey handed him the DMV records.

Looking over the list, he zeroed in on the one line that
had been both circled and highlighted.

"Dennis Hill," Matt said, the hair rising on his arms.

"According to the records, he owns a twelve-year-old
granite-crystal metallic Chevy Tahoe," Starkey said. "But
he's never mentioned it and has never driven it to work.
Like he's hiding it. He's already got a Jeep, and his wife
drives a sedan."

"Three vehicles," Matt said. "Tomlinson said that there
will be patterns of three's in the killer's life. Carl, grab his
personnel record."

Farran hurried out down the hall.

"What do you know about Dennis?" Matt asked Starkey. "Anything involving three's in his life."

"Um, well, he married his wife three times. Does that
count?"

"Why on earth would he marry her three times?" Kent asked.

"The first time was at the justice of the peace. Second was a big ceremony and reception. But his mother was sick or something. She's in the Silver Springs Nursing Home. The third time was over there so his mom could be a part of it. He's really proud of it, too. Celebrates three wedding anniversaries every year. His wife brags about how romantic he is."

Farran came back with the file.

Matt snatched it from his hands and opened it. Perusing it, he stopped midway. "He's got three kids, too."

"Oh yeah, he does." Starkey nodded. "Or did. I forgot. One of his daughters died. Meningitis, I think."

Matt looked for the date of death. "His daughter died three years ago. A month before the University Killer last struck. Hey, Kent. I need you to go to his house. Speak to his wife. See what she knows." He gave him the address. Hill lived in close proximity to the campus.

"Dennis has a son who attends the university," Starkey said. "Liam. We can find him at one of the frat houses. Alpha-something. He might know something, too."

Matt grabbed his hat and keys. "Let's find out."

Chapter Twenty-Two

Hannah stirred, her heavy eyelids lifting. Her throat was dry. Her mouth felt like cotton. She stared up at a low gray ceiling. Soft amber light came from a lamp somewhere. As she sat up, chains rattled. She realized she was on top of a bed. Full-size. Wrought iron frame.

Her wrists were now in front of her but still cuffed, with a long chain locked to the top of the bed frame. She gazed down at herself. Her clothes were gone, except for her bra and panties.

She stood, barefoot, more chains rattling, and swayed on her feet. There was an iron shackle around each ankle with a separate chain connected to one of the lower corners of the bed. Sickening awareness struck her that he'd restrained her in a manner to make spreading her legs easier.

Bile burned her throat, and her stomach clenched.

Where were her clothes? Her belt?

She looked around. The room was small. A cell, really. Made of concrete. Maybe nine by twelve. The bed took up most of the space.

In a corner sat a table no larger than a nightstand. With a lamp on top of it. Beyond the table was a door.

She shuffled forward, only to be snatched to a halt. The chain connected to her handcuffs wouldn't let her make it past the bed.

Kneeling down, she looked under the bedframe.

Her clothes—and a bucket, but she didn't want to think about what that was for. She reached for the pile of clothes and dragged it out. Everything was in tatters. He had cut her pants, jacket, top and belt into pieces. The only thing intact was the buckle.

The fool hadn't checked it. And she was going to use that mistake against him.

She pulled out the short blade and shoved everything else back under the bed.

As she stood, the room spun. Turning slowly, she gazed at the walls. When she faced the one behind the bed, she froze. Polaroid pictures of women, bruised and still—murdered—covered the concrete like some sick wallpaper. Her skin crawled.

Each photo was of a different blonde.

And there were more than twenty.

MATT STOOD INSIDE the foyer of the Alpha Theta Nu frat house alongside Sergeant Starkey, waiting for Liam.

His cell phone rang. "Granger," he said, answering.

"Bonnie Hill didn't answer the door," Kent said. "I looked around through the windows. Saw her unconscious on the couch. An open bottle of wine on the table. I kicked in the door. She's got a pulse, but I can't wake her. I think her husband drugged her. The ambulance is on the way."

"Okay. Search the house. See what you can find that might point to where he's taken Hannah."

"Will do. I'll keep you posted."

"What's up?" Starkey asked.

Matt was about to answer, but a tall kid—eighteen years old, with dark hair and dark eyes; a younger, fitter version of Dennis—came down the stairs.

"Hey, Sergeant Starkey." The young man looked at Matt. "Hi, I'm Liam."

"Chief Granger."

"I was told you needed to speak with me."

"Son, we're trying to locate your father," Matt said. "It's of the utmost importance that we find him. It's a matter of life or death."

"He should be at home. With my mom."

"We checked there," Matt said gently. "Your mother was found unconscious and in need of medical attention."

"Oh my God. I'll call my dad." He reached for his phone.

"Please, don't." Matt raised a palm. "We're still piecing things together, and it would be best if we spoke with your father first."

Liam's brow furrowed. "Is he in trouble? You don't think he did something to my mom, do you?"

"We're not jumping to any conclusions," Matt said, not wanting to make the kid defensive, since they needed his help. "But it's imperative that we find him and speak with him in person." He kept his voice patient, his tone soft. "Is there any place that you can think of where he might go? A favorite spot? Somewhere he feels safe."

Liam nodded. "My grandparent's cabin. It's in the woods. In Wayward Bluffs." He gave them the address.

"Thank you." Matt turned to Starkey. "Take his phone and keep him at the station. No phone calls. Make him comfortable and give him updates on his mother's condition."

Matt turned and dashed out the door, running to his truck.

Hang on, Hannah.

His prize should be bright eyed by now and no longer groggy. He'd given her plenty of time to recover. Their first time together, he wanted her wide awake and fiery.

He removed the padlock, stuck the key back in his pocket and opened the door to the shelter.

Ducking his head, he climbed down and closed the door behind him.

Chains rattled as Hannah Delaney scooted back on the bed, bringing her knees up to her chest like she was scared. But fire burned in her eyes.

Was she up to something?

"Rise and shine," he said in a singsong voice.

Leaning forward a bit, she gaped at him. "You?" she asked, shock thickening her voice.

She didn't see the forest for the trees. Just like Granger and every other police chief before him.

No more disguises needed. He'd not only gotten rid of the wig, mustache and fake contacts but also the toupee he wore on a daily basis to hide his receding hairline.

He smiled. "These are the rules by which you live." And eventually die. "You will call me *Master*," he said, and she narrowed her eyes to slits. "Only by pleasing me during our hookups will you get food and water. If you make me angry, you will be punished. I own you now. The sooner you accept this, the better. For you." He waited to see what kind of response he'd get.

Sometimes they sobbed. Sometimes they argued. Sometimes they tried to bargain, promising that their parents would pay him money if only he released them. Inevitably, whether in the beginning or at the end, they all begged for mercy.

But Hannah didn't utter a single word. She just stared

at him. If looks could kill, he would be ashes blowing in the wind.

He grinned.

She was strong and healthy and would last a long time. Longer than any other. Not mere hours or days but weeks. He was sure of it.

With her fighting spirit, he would have to hurt her. To teach her that she wasn't to try to hurt him. And in that lesson, she would also learn how glorious her pleasure could be after pain.

Like breaking in a wild horse, this would take a firm hand and patience on his part. He'd have to be careful, though. She was a threat, but only if he allowed her to be. Taming her would certainly be no easy task. He was up for the challenge.

She was special. Different. He would cherish her, even as he despised her.

Suddenly giddy, almost drunk with anticipation, he stepped to the foot of the bed. Watched her—his feral, quiet cat curled in on herself.

Grinning, he grabbed the chain connected to her right ankle and yanked it, forcing her leg to extend to the corner of the bed. He bent down and fixed one of the links on a hook on the floor to hold it in place.

As he stood, he sensed and then heard movement, the bedsprings creaking.

Hannah pounced forward like lightning and jammed something sharp in the back of his shoulder blade. Hot agony pierced him. But she didn't stop. She kept stabbing and slicing and drawing his blood while he tried to block her blows, howling and cursing in shock and pain.

He stumbled backward, away from the bed, out of her deadly reach.

Eyes full of rage, she was crouched, poised to lunge again, a blade in her hand covered in his blood.

Where had it come from? He'd been so careful.

"If you think I won't fight you until my last breath, then you had better think again! You took the wrong woman. Do you hear me, you sick, perverted monster?"

No. He took the right one. She was perfect. He liked it when they fought. When they struggled. "Breaking you will be that much sweeter. I think it's time for your first real lesson."

He stormed out of the shelter, leaving the door open. The cold night air would cool her off. He marched toward the cabin, realizing he'd forgotten to charge the cattle prod.

He swore to himself. While he had to wait for it to juice up, she would be that much weaker from the cold air, shivering, her teeth chattering, the deadly edge to her fighting drained.

But that wasn't enough punishment for Hannah Delaney. He was in agony.

Not only would he use the cattle prod, but he'd put her in a straitjacket, too. That would show her. Three days wearing that, and then she'd call him *Master*.

About a quarter of a mile down the road from the address Liam had given Matt, he pulled off to the side and shut the engine. From the back seat, he took a bulletproof vest, strapped it on and slipped his jacket over it. After he double-checked his Glock, he stuffed extra magazines, each containing fifteen rounds, into his pocket. He hooked two flash grenades on his vest, grabbed his night-vision goggles and flipped them down.

He set off into the woods, going the direction where the

cabin should be. His shoulder ached something awful, but he ignored the pain.

Steadily, carefully, he moved, scanning for movement or anything that might give away his presence. Such as flood-lights or security cameras. He spotted nothing. Kept going. Stayed alert. He slipped between the trees like a shadow.

In minutes, he came upon the back side of a cabin. He prayed that this was the right place and that Hannah was safe.

Footsteps pounded down wooded stairs at the front of the house.

Fifteen feet before the back porch, he cut quietly to the left, tracking the footfalls over dry leaves. He peeked around the side of the house.

A man stalked toward a mound.

Dennis Hill. Holding a straitjacket—the buckles flap-ping—and something else, like a metal stick, but then Matt noticed the familiar U-shaped tip. Sparks flared, tiny bright flashes on the faint green tinge of his screen.

A cattle prod!

Matt ripped off his night-vision goggles and took aim with his Glock.

But Dennis climbed down the stairs that led below ground, grabbing hold of the door to close it.

Right before it slammed shut, Matt heard Hannah swear-ing.

She was alive, and she was fighting. The icy fear that had squeezed his heart loosened its grip a little.

He rushed over to the mound. Took a flash grenade from his vest. Pulled the pin with his teeth. Cracked open the door. Tossed it in and shut the door.

A deafening boom erupted in tandem with a bright flash of light. It would incapacitate Hannah just as much as Dennis for a critical moment. But she would recover. The same couldn't necessarily be said about Dennis.

Matt threw open the door and hustled down the steps with his weapon at the ready.

The sight before him made his blood boil. Hannah was chained to a bed, writhing from the effects of the flash bang, bloody hands covering her ears and more blood splattered on her half-naked body.

Rage overwhelmed Matt. He charged Dennis, snatching him up from the floor, gritting his teeth through the sharp pain in his arm, and thrashed the man with his fist until blood ran from his nose.

Matt shoved him to the ground, face-first. Hard. He put a knee on his back, keeping him pinned, yanked Dennis's arms behind him and slapped cuffs on him tight.

Standing up, he spotted the straitjacket and cattle prod. He had half a mind to string Dennis up, use the cattle prod on him and then put an end to that brutal beast. But ranch justice, a quick death, was too good for him.

Matt kicked the cattle prod away. He looked up, and his gaze snagged on the concrete wall behind the bed covered in heinous photos. Renewed fury rushed over him, but he needed to help Hannah.

He went over to the bed, sat down and reached for her.

Still squirming, she lashed out with a blade that came dangerously close to his throat, but he'd been expecting anything and pulled back out of her reach.

He caught her wrists gently with one hand and pressed a palm to her cheek with the other. Her eyelids lifted, and her gaze found his.

Relief washed over her face. He hauled her up into his

arms, the chains jangling, and held her tight to his chest. Her cold body shivered against him.

He pulled back, took off his jacket and wrapped it around her.

"You're right in the nick of time," she said, her teeth chattering.

"I try to be punctual." Matt dug out a handcuff key from his pocket and freed her wrists. "There's so much blood on you."

"None of it's mine. It's his."

He got to work on the shackles on her ankles and released her. "You take too many chances."

She stood and rubbed her wrists. "Only when necessary."

He ripped the blanket from the bed and wrapped it around her waist. "You scared the hell out of me." He tugged her back into his arms, determined to never let her go.

Tipping her head up, she looked at him. "You say the most romantic things."

Epilogue

Hannah leaned against Matt, her head on his chest, his uninjured arm curled around her as they sat on his sofa in front of a cozy fire. She sipped her whiskey, grateful she'd made it out of Dennis Hill's lair alive. Relieved Zoey Williams was unharmed. Happy to have Matt at her side, willing to go into hell and fight the devil—not only with her but also *for* her.

Matt picked up her legs and draped them over his lap.

"I still can't wrap my mind around how many women Dennis Hill actually killed," she said, her skin crawling as she thought about the photos on the wall.

Twenty-four in total had been murdered. Hill had a type, and he never deviated from the profile. Young, under twenty-two, blond, fair skin, petite.

"If not for you, we never would have found his first twelve victims buried on the property of his cabin."

They'd thought Paige Johnson was his first victim, when in actuality, it was Nicole Noland.

"Agent Tomlinson was correct about the personal connection," Matt continued.

Nicole had dated Dennis when he was a kicker on the

SWU football team. Number thirty-three jersey. Nicole had broken up with him after they got into a car accident, and he injured his leg and couldn't play anymore. He started dating Bonnie, his current wife, and waited three months to rape and kill Nicole. He'd used Bonnie as his alibi.

Hannah shook her head, horrified by what Dennis had done to his victims and his family. "For twenty years, he's been drugging Bonnie, making that poor woman think she has a drinking problem, so he could sneak out and kill women. The shame his wife must've felt when you questioned her about her husband's whereabouts the night Madison Scott was murdered. Too embarrassed to say she was drunk and had blacked out and couldn't remember, even though she had really been roofied."

"Dennis fooled everyone. He was so unassuming, lurking right under the nose of every campus police chief for the past twenty years."

After he'd graduated from SWU, Dennis tried to join the campus police department, but his leg injury prevented him from passing the physical, and he became the office manager instead, picking his victims from the students who came into the police station to register their bicycles.

He confessed that nothing in particular had triggered this latest murder spree. Only that he'd felt compelled to find a sense of release.

"Promise me something," Matt said.

"What?"

"That you'll never lie to me again," he said, referring to her telling him that Kent had texted her. "No matter how difficult. No matter how complicated. Not even to protect me."

She would always do whatever she could to protect him. But she'd never lie to him again. "I promise. I'm sorry. You understand why?"

He nodded. There was no judgment or anger in his eyes. Only warmth. The knowledge that he understood her and accepted her, flaws and all, meant everything.

Matt rubbed her legs before taking her foot and massaging it.

"I should be massaging you." She kissed him on the lips, loving the feel of his stubble against her skin.

"You should, and you'll get your chance later, in the bedroom." He winked at her.

She couldn't help but smile.

He picked up his drink, took a swallow and went back to massaging her foot. "The university administration is impressed that we caught two serial killers."

Foster's DNA matched that of the Emerald City Butcher. Following a hunch, Kent had cadaver dogs search the state park situated in between the two spots where Dr. Bradford Foster liked to fish. They'd found four more bodies.

"Sam Lee will finally be released from prison," she said. "But nothing can restore the years stolen from him."

"At least his name will be cleared, and he can enjoy his freedom while knowing that the real Butcher will get what's coming to him."

Her thoughts careened back to Dennis Hill and his plans for her in that storm shelter. "I feel for Hill's children." His son, Liam, and older daughter, Susie. "And his wife."

She understood the unique agony of being the child of a serial killer. A nightmare she wouldn't wish on her worst enemy.

"Foster had kids, too."

It was hard to believe such men loved their children, their families, when they would leave them that legacy of evil.

"I have no control over what Erica Egan prints, but I have some influence with the campus paper. They've agreed to make it clear that the families of Hill and Foster didn't know the horrible truth and will ask for people to respect their privacy."

"That was really thoughtful of you."

He was the sweet one in this relationship.

"Hey." He picked up her hand and kissed her knuckles, and the tenderness in his eyes made her breath catch. "This might sound nuts or too fast, but what do you think about moving in here? Us making a home together?"

Stunned, she looked at him, totally blindsided and speechless.

"It's fast, but we both put in crazy hours on the job, and I do a lot of work on the ranch. It might be the only way to see each other with any sort of consistency. I want to build on this. This connection. And you said you were never sleeping in your place again."

And she wasn't.

When she didn't respond, he said, "I'm not trying to push."

"No. I want you to push. Sometimes we need a nudge out of our comfort zone for our own good." Funny how coming inches from being tortured and dying had made her realize how much was lacking in her life. "I want to be with you. See what *this* can grow into." Happiness swelled inside her as she studied his face.

The side of his mouth curved up. "Even if you fall madly in love and end up needing me?"

"I'm already falling, cowboy," she said, not mentioning how hard she was falling, and he smiled fully. "And as for needing you? I've learned that's not such a bad thing."

She'd needed him throughout this entire case, as well as the one they'd worked on last year. But she hadn't realized that she also needed his warmth, his understanding, his intensity.

His strength.

He leaned over and kissed her with tenderness and heat. This new relationship, this remarkable joy and lightness of being, was scary but wondrous. And worth it.

She smiled at him. "I guess you better get me a set of keys, because this is home."

* * * * *